# HAVOC ON A HOMEWRECKER

## Acknowledgements

To my Lord and Savior, thank you for your grace and mercy. Why you love me so, I truly will never know but I am thankful and humbled that you do.

To my parents Ray & Shirley: I love you, I love you, I love you. The two of you are exceptional and I know I was blessed with two of the best that were ever created.

To my family: The Leslies, Caudles, Turners, Masseys, and Walkers: I Love You! To my extended family & friends: I Love You! To Banita Brooks, I love you sis! To Robyn Traylor, JeaNida Luckie- Weatherall, Andrea Anderson, Denia Turner, Sheila Jones-Weathersby, Keisha Woods, Samantha Pettiway, Mary Green, Danielle Churcher –Straub, Malika Richards, Carlene Bowman, Jewel Horace, Ayanna Butler, Barbara Love, Karena Cowan, Shan Gradney, LaBrina Jolly, Althea JustBeing Me, Rhea Alexis M. Banks, Zakkiyah Karmel Hibbler, Susan Vincent, Me'Tova Hollingsworth, Camille Renee Lamb, Trenya Arrington, Timiska Martin-Webb, Natalia Powell, and each and every person who has shown me love and support by purchasing my books or just saying "Good Morning", Thank you! To everyone on the Love, Lies, and Lust fan page and my personal fan page: Thank you! To all the bookstores, clubs, and promoters that continue to support me and my work: Thank you!! To all the authors that show me love and support: Thank you!! To my editor: Thank you! To Hot Book Covers: Thank you! To the G Street Chronicles CEO Exclusive Readers, thank you for the support and entertainment! To the Just Read Book Club: there is never a dull moment and I love it!

To George Sherman Hudson, Shawna A., and the G Street

Chronicles family: Thank you & Much Love! If there is anyone I forgot please blame the voices in my head and not my heart. To every person with a hope, wish or dream: P.U.S.H.!

**"Sometimes a man's silence can be his biggest lie…"**

**~Mz. R**

For You…you know who you are…

~ Love & Kisses

G STREET CHRONICLES
A NEW URBAN DYNASTY
WWW.GSTREETCHRONICLES.COM

# Chapter 1

## Toi

I flipped open my compact, quickly checking my reflection in the mirror. I looked into my brown eyes. *Damn I'm fine*, I thought. I know what you're thinking, but please don't confuse my confidence with conceit. However, if you could see me right now—smooth, dark skin with high cheekbones, full lips, dark brown eyes with long, curly lashes and a 5'5" frame with a banging "you can tell she works out" body—you would agree. I smiled when I saw everything was as it should be—intact and fly—then dropped the compact back in my bag. I'd decided to wear my red wrap dress that stopped just above my knees for the evening, and the more I thought about it the more I was convinced it was an excellent choice. Not only did the dress have a V-neck that showed just a glimpse of my cleavage, it hugged my hips and complemented my behind perfectly. It was sexy but classy.

I tapped my heels under the table. I was as nervous as a virgin in bed with a man working with 12-inch wood as I waited for my boyfriend, Justin, to return from the men's room. All week leading up to tonight, Justin had been acting a little out of character. Don't get me wrong; he was still the loving and affectionate man I had come to know and love, but I kept getting the feeling that there was something on his mind. This morning I found out what when I stopped by his apartment with croissants and coffee for our daily breakfast ritual. The two of us engaged in light conversation throughout our meal but I could still sense something was on his mind. After breakfast, I was putting away dishes when I found a small, velvet-covered box stuffed at the back of the towel drawer. The same towel drawer that just yesterday contained nothing but towels. My curiosity got the best of me so I opened the box to find inside a beautiful, heart-shaped diamond with a vintage-style platinum band. Although the ring wasn't what I consider my taste—I always envisioned something a little flashier or better yet, bigger—it was beautiful and yes, it was an engagement ring!

The ring took me by surprise. Over the course of our three-year relationship, Justin and I discussed marriage and having children frequently and agreed that we wanted to have both, but we'd never had the discussion of when. However, I knew that family was as important to him as it was to me. The two of us had been taking our time, allowing the relationship to flow naturally, and things had been going along without a hitch. We had our disagreements, mainly about his desire to live together before marriage. I absolutely refused to shack up. If a man wanted to partake in my live-in benefits, then I needed to be his wife. Justin thought a bit more liberally; his parents had been shacking up for 20+ years. That might be good for his mama but it was definitely a no-go for me. During our disagreements about our living situation, there were moments when I wondered, *'Is he the guy?'* However, for me the good definitely outweighed the bad and I can say, *'Yes, he is'* without a doubt.

I still vividly remember the night we met. I was at the Green

Room with my two best friends, Anitra and LaShay. The three of us were getting it in on the dance floor, having a good time, and celebrating the weekend. Finding a man was the farthest thing from my mind, but when I looked across the dance floor and spotted the tall, dark-chocolate, beautiful specimen of a man staring at me, I felt compelled to introduce myself. After leaving the club, Justin and I had an early morning breakfast at IHOP, followed by our first official date later that day. After that first date we became practically inseparable, and we'd been together ever since.

I looked at my watch, wondering if something had happened to him. He'd been gone for well over ten minutes. I decided to keep waiting. Maybe I was just being impatient. Anxious about what was to come. When Justin asked me to meet him for dinner at Carrabba's, I knew that he was ready to pop the question. Carrabba's was our little spot for all things romantic. We came here for our first date, then four months later, we came here when Justin first told me he loved me. We even came here for dinner the night we first made love. It had become tradition for us to dine at the establishment only for special celebrations.

After waiting another ten minutes, I grabbed my bag and went to check on him. I'd heard of cold feet, but it was obvious Justin's had turned frigid. I had a waiter check the men's room, only to find it empty. I proceeded outside and found Justin in the parking lot engaged in what appeared to be a heated discussion with another woman. The woman was petite with short, layered hair, and a caramel complexion. She stood with one hand on her hip and the other pointed at Justin. She wore shorts that barely covered her coochie and a white tank top with the word BITCH printed in bright red letters across her breasts.

"I'm not playing with you, Justin," she continued to rant as

I approached. "This is your last…" She stopped when she saw me coming.

"Is that her?" she asked, nodding in my direction.

Justin looked over his shoulder at me quickly, then turned back around, mumbling something lowly.

"You better handle that shit," she said, folding her arms across her small breasts and looking in my direction. When Justin turned around a second time, he stared at me directly in the eyes.

"What's going on?" I asked, stopping in front of him.

"Toi, I was just on my way back in," he said quickly.

"You never answered the question," I reminded him. I looked past him at the chick throwing me glares from hell. "What's going on?"

"Toi, I—," he stuttered.

"Justin, you need to keep it one hundred," she said, cutting him off. "Ain't no time like the now." I wondered what proud institution could take credit for her fine lack of vocabulary.

"Justin, who is she?" I questioned. I was trying my best to remain calm. I knew in my heart that any explanation Justin provided was not going to weigh well in my favor, but I still wanted to give him and his little hood rat the benefit of the doubt.

"Toi," he said, putting his hands up. "Just give me another minute. Please." He looked like he wanted to cry. *Hell, no!* I felt my blood pressure rise in less than sixty seconds. Now I wanted an answer and I wanted it *right* now!

"Your minute is up," I said, pissed. "Who in the hell is she?"

Justin rubbed a hand across his forehead while exhaling deeply. He was stalling, wasting time. *Are you serious?* I asked myself.

"Answer the question, Justin," she said, smacking her lips. "Tell her who I is."

"Peaches!" he snapped, spinning around to look at her.

*Peaches? What kind of name is Peaches?* I thought.

"Can you be quiet for just a second? Please!"

Peaches lowered her eyes at him, frowning.

"Naw, fucks that!" she snapped, rolling her neck. "You had four months! I'm tired of playin' wit you." She stepped past him, looking at me with wide eyes. "Justin and me is together."

I stared at her. She was cute, I gave her that, but she couldn't possibly be Justin's type. Justin was a business owner and a shirt-and-tie kind of brother. She looked more like a video hoe, minus the video.

"Together?" I asked sarcastically. "You can't be serious."

"Tell her, Justin." Peaches egged him on, staring at him. "Tell her."

He loosened the silk tie he wore while shaking his head back and forth. No the hell he didn't, I thought.

"I'm waiting," I snapped. I placed one hand on my hip and extended the other out to my side, ready to go into "slap the shit out of him" mode.

"Toi, I'm sorry," he began. He looked at me with apologetic eyes. "I didn't mean for you to find out like this, but Peaches and I are together."

I looked at Peaches. The look of victory on her face was compelling me to slap the hell out of her, but I refrained. Besides, she was not my problem. Granted, she'd been involved with someone who I thought was my man, but my issue was not with her. Justin and I were in the relationship and he was the one who held an obligation to me, not Peaches.

"Since when, Justin?" I questioned.

"Off and on for eight months," he said lowly.

"You've been cheating on me for eight months?" I asked, raising my voice. "Why didn't you tell me you wanted someone else? You could have told me from day one, Justin. That's something I could have respected. Instead, you bring me to our restaurant and I have to find out from this hoe?"

"Who you callin' a hoe?" Peaches jumped in. She took a step toward me and Justin immediately stepped in between us. I stepped to the side so Peaches could still see me. I gave her a look that told her not to take my looks and class for weakness.

"Who do you think?" I asked, looking at her. "You are the hoe and obviously one who doesn't understand proper English. Hoe!"

Peaches began to rant and rave while waving her hands in the air. "You don't know me," she babbled. "I will fuck you up."

Every word that followed after that sounded like *blah, blah, blah,* to me. I was no longer listening to nor interested in what Peaches had to say. I was too busy staring at the heart-shaped diamond on her ring finger.

"Peaches!" I heard Justin say, breaking my trance. I looked around and saw that there were a few people passing by, watching the three of us. I felt a rush of embarrassment as I realized what should have been a private moment was turning into a public spectacle. I turned and walked away as Justin continued his attempt to calm down Peaches. My heart was beating a mile a minute as I began to process everything that was happening.

"Oh, so now you chasin' after her, Justin?" I heard Peaches yelling behind me.

"Toi!" Justin called my name. His voice was growing closer, my clue that he was following me.

I reached my car and quickly unlocked the doors. I climbed behind the wheel, slamming the door. What just happened? I asked myself. A few seconds later Justin stood outside my car, tapping the driver's side window.

"Toi, let me talk to you," he practically begged. "Please, Toi. I'm sorry."

I started the engine of my Camry, then lowered my window.

"I didn't want you to find out like this," he explained. "I—"

"I found a ring in the towel drawer this morning," I informed him. "Is that the ring she has on her finger?" I stared straight ahead, looking out the windshield. I couldn't bring myself to look at him.

"Toi, I—"

"Is that the ring?" I demanded, gripping the steering wheel tightly.

He paused, then exhaled. "Yes."

"You proposed to her?" I questioned.

"Toi, yes, but I—"

"You what?" I yelled. "We were supposed to get married. We've always talked about marriage and starting a family. Us, Justin."

"Yes, we've talked about getting married," he said slowly. "But we never said we were going to marry each other."

*Come again?* I thought. "What?" I asked, finally forcing myself to look at him. I stared at him in disbelief. I thought some things were just understood. One of them being that if you're discussing marriage with your girlfriend, it's because you plan to marry that girlfriend someday. Justin had just informed me that I was wrong.

"Toi, I asked Peaches to marry me today at lunch," he advised me. "I've been trying to tell you about her for a while now but I didn't know how."

"How about, I'm in love with another woman!" I yelled. "What's wrong with that? That would have worked for me!" Justin could have chosen any method he desired as long as he chose one.

"It's not that easy," he said, standing with his hands in his pockets.

"I thought you loved me," I said. I was becoming more and more emotional. I could feel myself on the verge of tears and the last thing I wanted to do was cry, especially considering Peaches was still standing in the parking lot watching us.

"I do love you," he said. "But—"

"But what?" I asked, cutting him off. "What?"

"Peaches is different," he said.

I wanted to say 'Yeah, ghetto,' but I refrained.

"She's exciting and fun," he continued. "Plus—"

"So, you cheated on me because you think I'm boring?" I interrupted.

"You're predictable," he said. "I mean you're a great woman but predictable..."

"That's something that can be changed," I said. "Easily—"

"It's not just that," he said. "Toi, Peaches is pregnant. Four months."

I'll confess: until that very moment, thoughts of Justin and I working through this situation danced in my head, right along with thoughts of how I could get even. It was selfish and immature, but it was true. I loved him so much that I could overlook the obvious foolery of his cheating, and even overlook the embarrassment I felt from the scene we'd caused in front of spectators leaving the restaurant. Still, my forgiveness would come with consequences—the consequence of payback. Just because I granted forgiveness did not mean he would not reap the same bullshit he sowed. Regretfully, there was no getting past this one.

"You got her pregnant?" I asked. I was in utter disbelief. "So not only are you a lying, cheating-ass dog but you're a stupid one at that." Justin looked slightly shocked by my choice of words. I normally kept myself poised with a certain amount of grace but screw that; my grace went out the window when he announced that he was having a baby with the hood rat.

"Toi, it was an accident that I'm trying to make right," he said. "You have to respect that."

"You're out of your damn mind if you think I respect that you were running up in that bitch raw while you were with me!" I yelled. "Fuck you, Justin!"

"Toi—" he didn't get the opportunity to finish his sentence. I shifted into drive, then peeled off. I whipped out of the parking lot with tears streaming down my face.

*'Peaches is pregnant…she's exciting and fun…you're predictable…"* Justin's words hurt me over and over, echoing through my mind. I decided to go back and let him know exactly how I felt. I cut my wheel to the left, making a U-turn in the middle of the street. I made it back to the restaurant in what felt like a blink of an eye.

Justin was walking across the parking lot with his back to me. He was walking toward his car and appeared to be oblivious to his surroundings. There was no sign of Peaches. I pulled into the parking lot and slammed on my brakes, bringing my car to a sudden halt. I was hurt, and still shocked by how Justin had played me. And he expected me to be all right with it? Really? I slowly eased on the gas. As I drove toward Justin, I thought of all the times we had made love. I could barely feel Justin when he was inside of me, and he had the nerve to cheat on *me*? I increased my speed as I approached him.

"Predict this bitch!" I said aloud.

He turned around, looking over his shoulder and finally facing me. I could see his face through the glare of my headlights; he looked scared shitless. I thought about his body rolling in the air as I hit him doing 50MPH.

G STREET CHRONICLES

A NEW URBAN DYNASTY

WWW.GSTREETCHRONICLES.COM

# Chapter 2

# Toi

Two years later...

"You have a glass break here, there, and in that far left corner," Dallas said, flashing her green eyes at me. She continued to give me details on Fashionista's security system and motion detectors as we stood at the store's entrance. Fashionista was a specialty retailer that sold brand-name ladies' clothing at lower prices. I had been working for the retailer for six months as a sales associate, and recently received a promotion. I was going to manage my own store. The store was small, only four employees, but I didn't care; it was mine. My boss said in the company's 20-year history, I was the first associate to go directly from the sales floor to management. I was humbled and honored, but I also knew that busting my butt in my previous position got me where I was now standing.

I was grateful, and ecstatic at how well things had turned around for me in the past few months. I won't lie; my journey was more than bumpy and it almost landed me behind bars. The night Justin dumped me, I had my foot on the gas and visions of him rolling up and over the hood of my car. I was in my zone until someone—I like to say it was my guardian angel—spoke to me and told me not to do it. I cut my wheel to the right and barely missed him. I lost control of the car and ended up slamming it into the side of a parked vehicle.

Justin was unharmed and I managed to avoid a murder charge; however, the police arrested me for reckless driving. I could have served at least five days in jail with a fine, but instead the judge let me off with just a $500 fine. To my delight, Justin was the only witness present and frankly, he saved my ass. He advised the police that I was not intentionally trying to hurt him and that he witnessed me trying to stop my car. I know I would not have been so lucky if Peaches had been present. I was sure she would have told a very different story and the sad part is, her version probably would have been true. I hadn't seen Justin since we went to court and I figured it was for the best. After all, I had made a vow that if God got me off without serving time I would never touch the man again. I planned to keep that vow.

My drama with Justin wasn't the only hard hit I took that year: two months after the breakup, I lost my job when my customer service position with AT&T was eliminated. I had been with the company for four years, but it took them less than 60 seconds to tell me and 15 of my coworkers, that they were closing the office here in Huntsville, Alabama and we were no longer needed. It took me a year to find my position with Fashionista, and that was only after lowering my standards. I went from making $17 an hour to minimum wage. I had to go to my father for a loan just to pay my rent and prevent the dreaded alternative of my moving to Texas to live with him and my mother. I was taking one hit after another.

At the time, it felt like everyone and everything I had been loyal to had abandoned me. However, things slowly began to look up and now I was here, making three dollars more than I did at AT&T. Plus, as a store manager I would now receive a monthly bonus. I had a new car and I was saving, working toward buying my first house. In addition to all that, I had a new attitude and was focused on myself.

What I didn't have was a man, and I was fine with that. If it happened it happened, but I wasn't trippin' if it didn't. Now that my career was back on track, I planned to focus on establishing myself with the company and seeing how far it would take me. Also, I liked having my time to myself. No checking in. No answering questions. None of that extra BS that becomes a distraction. I've learned that distractions can cost you money, and I'm all about my paper. Don't get me wrong if someone in tune with what I had going on came along then so be it, but I was definitely not looking.

*****

An hour after my tour, I walked the sales floor greeting customers and ensuring that everything was flowing smoothly. The doorbell rang, indicating someone was at the back door. I excused myself to answer the ringing bell. A moment later I opened the door for a tall, good-looking brother with brown skin, low-cut hair, and a lean build, who stood outside holding a large box. He wore a blue khaki shirt with matching shorts; the typical uniform for Alliance Express, or A-Ex, a local delivery service. He looked like he was either depressed or tired as hell. He'd parked his truck in the alley, blocking the fire lane.

"Hello," I said. I stepped outside to hold the door open for him.

"Hey," he said. He carried the box in and sat it down on the concrete stockroom floor. "I have five more for you."

"Okay," I said, pushing the door back until it remained open without my assistance. "But next time you may want to park in the front, so that you won't block the alley."

"The manager asked me to park back here," he said. "She said she didn't want me dragging boxes through the front of her store."

I knew he was referring to Cassie, the manager I had replaced. I could understand her point, considering the back entrance led directly to the stockroom; however, I didn't want to experience any problems in the event the fire marshal rolled through or there was an emergency. I knew I wouldn't be the one held responsible, but I still wanted to be considerate of the stores surrounding me.

"I'm the manager now," I explained. I watched him as he dropped the fifth box on the floor. "So it's okay for you to deliver in the front."

He looked annoyed as he handed me the electronic scanner used to capture my signature. "I'll remember that." *Was that attitude?* I asked myself. I decided to brush it off as his having a bad day.

"Thanks," I said, pleasantly.

"Yeah," he said quickly, before exiting through the open door and climbing back into the delivery truck.

"You're welcome," I said aloud, shaking my head at his rudeness. I noticed the gathering of gray clouds in the sky overhead. It looked like it was going to rain. *Maybe that was his problem,* I thought to myself. He probably was so focused on trying to get his route completed before he got caught in the rain that good customer service was the last thing on his mind. Regardless, the only thing I couldn't stand more than a lying man was one who gave me attitude for no reason.

# Chapter 3

## Lisa

The grandfather clock sitting in the corner of my living room chimed, informing me that it was now 9:00. I could hear the rain outside as it beat like drums, bouncing off the gutters of the house. I sat wondering where my husband Carlton was and exactly what he was doing. When I spoke to him earlier he advised me that he was running behind on his deliveries, but I informed him that I needed him home by eight so that he could help get our son ready for bed. I had a terrible headache and I needed my husband, my partner, to have my back in performing the nightly duties. However, he still hadn't made it home yet and now it was an hour past CJ's bedtime. I was getting sick and tired of Carlton's shit, coming home late from work with the same old tired excuses.

"We were shorthanded...Such and such went on vacation... They doubled my load..."

I had them all memorized and I could hear them echoing in my head. I pulled on the belt of the plush robe I was wearing, securing it tightly around my waist. *Why is he trying me?* I questioned myself. *I knew he could be home by now, that's if he wanted to be. He's probably out doing only God knows what*, I thought. You would think that after being together for six years, Carlton would know what *not* to do to piss me off. Yet once again here I was, mad as hell!

Lately, it seemed that everything Carlton did was meant to piss me off, as if his sole purpose for breathing was to start arguments with me. It wasn't always like that. When Carlton and I first started dating, he was the most charming and disciplined man I'd ever met. When I say disciplined, I mean he was patient. The kind of man who, when you tell him he wasn't getting any of the honeypot, accepted it without trying to persuade you otherwise. He was a real man, the kind of man who held doors open for me and pulled out chairs, who paid for everything, and was offended when I tried to reach for my purse to handle the check. Because of the way he treated me, I knew by our third date that Carlton was the man I wanted to marry and that someday I *would* be his wife by any means necessary. Why wouldn't I? Carlton believed that a man should be the head of his household and I played right along with him. The truth is, I believed a man should be the breadwinner, bill payer, and weight carrier, but the woman should always be the one with all the power. The first three years of our relationship were nearly perfect until I gave birth to our son; then things started going downhill. I instantly felt like Carlton no longer cared about my thoughts or feelings—as if I was no longer good for him and he only wanted me around to raise our child.

The sound of the front door unlocking stopped my reminiscing and dropped me back smack-dab in reality. I slid my feet into slippers I kept on the carpeted floor in front of me. Leaning forward on the sofa I took a deep breath. Carlton stepped through the door and immediately locked eyes with mine. *Yeah, trick*, I said silently. I had our furniture arranged so that when the front door opened, the first thing he saw when he stepped over the threshold was the sofa and me.

Carlton looked like he wanted to say something but he didn't. Instead, he eased past me and headed toward our bedroom. I quietly followed behind him, waiting until we were in the privacy of our bedroom to confront him.

"Where the hell you been?" I asked, watching Carlton as he removed his shirt.

"I told you I was running behind," he said calmly. I watched him as he eased down onto the bed, then kicked off his shoes one at a time.

"I thought I told you to leave those funky-ass shoes outside at the door," I said, rolling my eyes. "And don't sit on my clean bed with your dirty-ass clothes."

He stood up, then began to unbutton his shorts. I watched him as he removed his remaining clothing piece by piece until he was butt naked. After doing so he walked off and headed toward our master bathroom.

"I like how you just leave your shit lying here for me to pick up after your ass!" I snapped. I bent down, slowly picking up the items one by one. "Do you even care how hard I work to maintain this home?" Sometimes he was so inconsiderate.

He ignored my question as he closed the bathroom door behind him. I stood in awe as I heard the shower running from the other side of the bathroom door. I hated to be ignored but I decided to let it slide. I marched out of our bedroom with Carlton's clothes and shoes in my hands while trying to calm my nerves. I dropped his things on the floor of our laundry room, then began sorting through the pile. The sound of our home phone ringing halted my stride. I quickly grabbed the cordless off the kitchen counter.

"Hello," I answered, balancing the phone on my shoulder.

"Hey, Lisa."

"Hey, Martha," I replied, rolling my eyes. Martha was Carlton's friend Gabe's great-aunt, but she treated and claimed Carlton as one of her own. She was almost 70, a widow, and constantly in need of something. I knew if she was calling there was either something she wanted, or someone was having something at her church. I got so tired of hearing how I needed to fellowship with her. At that point I really didn't care why Martha was calling, I just wanted her to state her point and get off my phone.

"I'm not going to hold you," she said slowly. "I just wanted to thank Carlton for coming to my rescue."

"What do you mean?" I asked, curious.

"My car stopped on the way back from the church," she explained. "And he came and gave me a jump. I was glad too, because Gabe wasn't answering his phone and…"

I listened as Martha rambled on about how Carlton had not only given her car battery a jump start, but he'd followed her home too, and waited until Gabe finally arrived. He couldn't do one little thing I asked, but let his friends or family call and he goes above and beyond the call of duty? Okay.

"Tell him I said thank you again," Martha finally said. "And I hope to see y'all Sunday. Night."

"Night, Martha," I said, before slamming the phone down. Carlton choosing to put his outside family first was another complaint I had about him. His friends or Martha could call and he would drop whatever he was doing without a second thought. Meanwhile, it seemed I always had to play the waiting game with him. Yet I'm the one raising his child and making sure the roof over his head remains neat and clean?

"Ungrateful ass…," I mumbled to myself. I marched back into our bedroom and found Carlton sitting on the bed, rubbing lotion over his arms and biceps. He wore a pair of dark-blue boxers and a gray wife beater. He looked clean and refreshed, as if he didn't have a care in the world while I, his wife, was stressed out and pissed off.

"You saw Martha tonight?" I questioned, folding my arms across my chest. "And don't lie because I just got off the phone with her."

He looked at me, then shook his head. "Then why even ask the question?" he asked sarcastically.

"Because I felt like it," I said with an attitude. "Because I asked you to be here at a specific time and you couldn't do that for me, but when Martha called you were probably happy to run to her rescue. That's why."

"First of all," he began, "I didn't get back to the warehouse until 7:45, so I still wouldn't have made it here by 8:00 pm. Secondly, I wasn't going to leave my aunt stranded in the rain on the side of the road." He looked at me, frowning, then stood and walked past me, out the bedroom door.

"Why couldn't you call me?" I asked. I followed him into the kitchen. "What's wrong with showing me some damn courtesy? Huh? You couldn't call me and let me know where you were at?"

"What difference would it have made?" he asked. He opened the refrigerator door, pulling out a plate of chopped steak and potatoes I had prepared earlier that evening. "Either way, you would have reacted like you're doing now." He removed the plastic wrap, sliding the plate inside the microwave and setting the cook time.

"You don't know how I would have reacted," I said defensively. "You didn't give me a chance."

Carlton walked over to the kitchen table and sat down. "It's damned if I do and dammed if I don't with you," he said nonchalantly. "That much I do know. So, again, what difference would it have made?"

"All I know is that as a man you should have checked in on your wife and son before you did anything else. A real man would have."

He looked at me, smirked, then laughed.

"Oh, that shit's funny?" I asked. The timer dinged on the microwave. I marched over to the counter before he had time to get up. I flung the door of the microwave open, then grabbed the plate. "Next time, eat with your aunt." I pressed the lid opener on the trash can and dumped the contents, along with the plastic plate, in the trash. "Ha, ha," I said sarcastically.

I looked at him, daring him to say something to me. He didn't. Instead, he rose from the table and walked away. I was fuming from his lack of emotion. It was obvious to me that he just didn't care. I stood in the kitchen alone and angry.

A minute later Carlton returned in the hallway dressed in a Nike T-shirt, sweats, and sneakers. He had his keys in one hand and his cell phone in the other as he walked toward the front door.

"Where you going?" I asked, walking toward him.

"Out, to get some air," he said.

"No, you're not," I said. "We are going to talk about this. Right now."

"Talk for what?" he asked. "Whenever we talk it always leads to an argument. I'm not going to argue with you." He reached out to put his hand on the doorknob. I stepped in between him and the door, blocking his path.

"Move, Lisa," he said, stepping back to look at me.

"I told you, you're not going anywhere," I said, angry. "You're so selfish and inconsiderate."

"All right," he said, shaking his head. "Whatever you say."

He was taunting me on purpose. Carlton knew exactly what to do and say to push my buttons.

"Now move," he ordered.

"Why?" I asked, stepping toward him. "You running late? Is that bitch waiting?" I had no fear or concern that my husband was cheating. I only threw out the 'other woman' thing out of anger, to piss him off. The proper response to this would have been "No," but I told you Carlton liked to try me.

"Whatever," he said.

In my mind and within my emotions I heard, "Yeah, she's waiting." That only added fuel to my internal fire. I reached down, attempting to grab his keys. "You won't see her tonight," I ranted. "I bet you that." Carlton snatched his arm back, causing me to miss and further pissing me off.

"Chill," he said.

"Go to hell!" I screamed. I could feel my heart pounding in my chest as the beats echoed in my ears. I felt hot as anger coursed through my veins. I began to swing my arms and fists wildly.

"Lisa," he called. "Stop it!"

"I fucking hate you!" I screamed. "You make me sick!" Carlton managed to block my swings until CJ appeared in the hallway.

"Daddy," he said.

I had been so lost in my own world, fueled by my own anger, that I hadn't noticed my son watching me. I redirected my attention to our three-year old standing in the hallway in his Iron Man pajamas. His big brown eyes were full of confusion as he rubbed the curly locks of hair on top of his head. Carlton let down his guard, also looking at CJ.

I smirked to myself as I suddenly swung my fist, landing a blow directly to his face.

"What in the hell is wrong with you?" he yelled, redirecting his attention to me and grabbing me by both wrists. The pressure from his grasp caused my wrists to sting and burn as he pushed me backward, slamming me against the door.

"Don't you ever do that shit again," he grunted through clenched teeth. Carlton stared at me with low, anger-filled eyes. I had never seen him so furious. I could tell he wanted to hit me. I could see the longing and desire etched in his eyes.

"Daddy," CJ repeated.

Carlton looked at me again, then released his grip on me. He walked over to our son and lifted him into his arms. "It's okay, buddy," he said, rubbing CJ's back. "Everything is okay."

I huffed as Carlton carried him down the hall and the two of them disappeared behind CJ's bedroom door. He's probably in there right now making me out to be the bad guy, I thought to myself. Hell, he probably *does* have another woman waiting on him!

I rubbed my wrists while thinking about what had just taken place between my husband and me. I was livid! I stared at my wrists, studying the red blotches from Carlton's hands. They were quickly turning an unattractive shade of blue and I knew they would be black by morning. I walked over to the kitchen counter, then picked up the cordless phone. I pressed the numbers on the key pad so hard I broke a nail.

"911, what is your emergency?" the dispatcher asked from the other end of the phone.

# Chapter 4

## Toi

Taking over as manager where someone else left off had its good points and its bad ones. I loved that my staff was already trained to do the basic mechanics of the job, but I hated that they had habits and practices that I found completely unprofessional. One of these habits was eating on the sales floor. I was walking through the store gathering pieces to dress a mannequin when I caught Chloe, one of my sales associates, standing behind the markdown table with a two-piece chicken meal sitting in front of her and a biscuit in between her lips.

"Cassie always let us eat on the floor when we didn't have customers," she explained, after I broached the subject. She covered her mouth as she chewed. "I assumed you would follow the same policy."

"No," I said, staring into her brown eyes. "Eating on the sales floor is strictly prohibited, and the only times I allow my employees to eat is during their scheduled breaks and lunches. The exception to that rule would be if you have a medical emergency or condition that requires you to eat outside of those times. And then the two of us can work out how many breaks are needed."

I watched as Chloe rubbed her hands together, knocking crumbs from her fingertips. I stared at the food remnants falling to the floor. *I hope she knows she is cleaning that up*, I thought to myself.

"The additional breaks will be without pay," I continued. I felt it was necessary for me to stress that point before she had any ideas to lie or attempt to take advantage of my kindness. "However, if you need them we can definitely work them in. Is there a personal problem that you'd like to make me aware of?"

"No," she said, shaking her head as her pale white skin turned an embarrassing shade of pink.

"Good," I said firmly. "Please take the rest of your meal into the break room."

"Okay," she said, folding the flaps of the box closed.

"Oh, and Chloe—make sure you sweep up those crumbs," I added.

She looked like she wanted to say something but she knew better. I planned to make sure all of my employees knew that I was sweet, but I wouldn't tolerate any bullshit.

Another challenge I faced as manager was the solicitation happening in front of the store. There was a representative from every industry—from music to clothes to books—in front of Fashionista every day. There was one man in particular who had become a problem. I first noticed him one afternoon when I was returning from lunch. He was speaking with two of my regular customers, showing them a few handbags. The next time I noticed him, I was dressing a mannequin in the window. He stopped a customer who had just purchased a pair of heels from one of my sales associates. After the man showed her his merchandise, she came back into the store and asked for a full refund, only to buy a similar item from the man outside. I could respect his hustle, but I couldn't respect that he was taking money out of my pockets!

I had just finished verifying Chloe had taken care of her mess when I saw the man in the parking lot. He stood by a baby-blue BMW, talking on the phone. I told my employees that I'd be back, then excused myself from the store.

"Hello," I smiled politely, approaching the man.

"Let me call you back," he said before flipping his phone closed. "Hello."

"I'm Toi Underwood," I advised him. "And I'm the new store manager here."

"It's nice to meet you Toi," he said. "Truly a pleasure." He lowered his eyes while looking from my eyes down to my toes then up again.

"Um, yeah," I said sarcastically. "Listen, I'm going to ask you to refrain from pushing your merchandise in front of my store."

He smiled, cocking his head to the side. "Now I'm sure there's something the two of us can work out, pretty lady. Something beneficial to the both of us."

"I doubt it," I replied. "So I'm going to need you to relocate, take your business elsewhere." I felt I was being pleasant but firm with the man. I didn't want to come off as a total hard-ass, but he needed to know I was serious.

"I tell you what," he said. "Why don't I move farther out into the parking lot. Give you a little more space. Respect your territory until you invite me in." He smiled, revealing a perfect set of teeth.

"Why don't I call the police?" I asked, batting my eyes at him. There was no rhyme nor reason for the two of us to continue our discussion. It wasn't up for debate and even if it had been, I didn't have the time. He nodded his head.

"No need for all that," he said. "You take care and God bless." I watched him as he climbed behind the wheel of the BMW, then drove off.

*****

The doorbell rang, indicating we had a delivery. I looked at my watch wondering who it possibly could be. For the past week A-Ex had been delivering before we opened. This worked out perfectly for me; I could get some of our new pieces out on the floor before I got bombarded with guests. That week, I was also pleasantly surprised to see that I had a new driver. The new driver, who introduced himself as Fred, was a short, olive-colored man with red hair. He was friendly and professional. I assumed the brother with the attitude I dealt with my first day was a substitute, or he had gotten fired.

When Fred didn't come that morning, I assumed I wasn't scheduled for deliveries. When I opened the door and saw Mr. Attitude, I was beyond disappointed.

"Where's Fred?" I asked, watching him as he unloaded box after box.

"He was just filling in for me," he said over his shoulder.

I wanted to yell, *Well, can he come back?*. Instead I said, "Oh." I was trying hard to hide my disappointment. "So, you were on vacation?" I was attempting to be courteous before giving him a reminder that I did not want him delivering at the back of the store.

"Nope," he said, flatly. There was an uncomfortable silence between the two of us. I decided my attempt at pleasant conversation was getting me nowhere.

"Just a reminder," I said, nicely. "Please come through the

front door next time. If you don't mind."

"I forgot," he said, handing me the scanner to sign. "I'll do that next time." He stood waiting for me to sign for the boxes. I decided to hit him with my second request while the getting was good.

"And if it's not a problem," I said, handing him the scanner. "Can you come before ten? Fred did and it worked out well for me."

He frowned while rubbing his brow with his hand.

"So, you want me to rearrange my entire route for you?" he asked. He stood with one hand in his pocket and a look of annoyance in his eyes. I was starting to think that my last request may have been the straw that broke the man's back. "Anything else I can do to make things more convenient for *you*? Anything?"

*A little less attitude*, I thought to myself.

"That should do it," I said, laughing lightly and trying to lighten the mood.

"Sorry," he said coldly. "It's more convenient for *me* to leave things like they are." He turned, then walked to the door. "Any other requests?" he asked, with his back to me.

"I guess not," I said.

He didn't respond. Instead he exited, leaving me slightly speechless.

# Chapter 5

## Toi

It was the weekend so I decided to step out for the night. It had been a long time since I got together with my besties and in my opinion, we were long overdue for a girls' night out. I no longer patronized the Green Room (for reasons I'm sure you understand), so the three of us agreed to meet at Shooter's, a local pool hall. I stepped in Shooter's a little after ten, carrying a clutch and wearing dark fitted jeans; a green, one-shoulder, vintage light-knit top; and bright yellow stilettos. I had been wearing suits and my hair pinned up for the last two weeks; it finally felt good to rock a pair of jeans and literally let down my hair. I felt sexy but comfortable and I was ready to have a good time.

I spotted my girls sitting at a high table in the back of the crowded room. LaShay was the first to notice me. She smiled, then waved her hand in the air. Her short, bright red, naturally curly hair glowed under the dim light hanging above the table. LaShay was a plus-size beauty with light skin, big brown eyes, and an aura that commanded your attention when she entered a room. She wore a light denim, button-front dress with wedges that tied around her ankles. Anitra sat to her left. Anitra was a little more conservative with her look but still beautiful in my opinion. She had cinnamon-colored skin with jet-black hair she kept in a mid-length bob, and a medium build. She wore a gray tank top and black shorts with heels.

The sound of Future's "Go Harder" pumping through the surround system made it seem like the artist was in the hall performing the track. The sounds of pool sticks tapping against pool balls and the chatter and laughter of other patrons commingled throughout the room.

"Hey chick." LaShay smiled as I approached the table. "Long time no see."

"Hey hunni." I smiled, then gave her a sisterly hug.

"Looking good, Toi." Anitra smiled, extending her arms to me. I walked past LaShay to hug her.

"You too," I said sincerely, easing into the empty chair that faced them.

"What's up with the two of you?" I asked.

"My blood pressure," Anitra said. She lifted the glass sitting on the table in front of her, took a sip, then sat the glass back down. "Kelvin is getting on my last damn nerve!"

"What else is new?" I teased, while looking around.

I tried to find a server so that I could order a drink. Watching LaShay and Anitra sip theirs had me thirsty.

"I'm serious, Toi," Anitra said. "I've already called *Divorce Court.* I'm too tired of his ass."

I redirected my attention to her, then frowned. Anitra and her husband Kelvin had been together close to ten years. The two of them were constantly arguing about any and everything you could think of, and Anitra claimed to be done with him at least once every other week. The truth was, they truly loved each other and probably would die before they let each other go. I think the arguments kept it interesting and made for even better makeups.

They were the cutest and possibly the most dysfunctional couple I knew.

"What has Kelvin allegedly done this time?" I questioned.

"What do you mean *allegedly*?" Anitra asked, her eyes wide. "Are you implying that I'm a drama queen who only thinks her man is wrong?"

"You are," LaShay jumped in. I watched as she finished off the contents in her glass. I nodded my head in agreement.

"I'm going to get me some real friends," Anitra commented, putting her hands up in mock frustration. "Some that understand me and can feel my pain. As soon as I do I'm cutting off you two heifers."

"Umm hum," LaShay mumbled. "Where in the hell is that skinny broad" she asked, looking around.

"The server?" I asked.

"Yeah, we haven't seen her since we first sat down," LaShay commented. "I need a refill."

"I'm good," Anitra said. "I don't need Kelvin taking advantage of me tonight. Although, I may have to do something to him as soon as I get home." In an instant she had forgotten her so-called drama with Kelvin.

"TMI," LaShay said, shaking her head. "TMI."

"I'm going to go to the bar," I said, standing up. "What are you drinking?" I asked LaShay.

After getting her order I waited in line at the bar. The thin brunette bartender looked like she was completely stressed out as she ran from one end of the bar to the other.

"What can I get for you?" she finally asked me.

"CÎROC and lemonade," I said. "And a Hennessy and coke, please." I was hoping she wouldn't play me on my drink. The last thing I wanted was a watered-down cocktail, especially considering I hadn't had a good drink in months.

"Here you go, babe." She smiled. "You want me to start you a tab?" I didn't plan on drinking more than just the one drink and possibly two, but I decided to keep my options open.

"Sure," I said. I was headed back to the table, where LaShay could now be seen rotating her hips and singing along to Estelle's "Thank You" that had just come on through the speakers.

I was so busy watching and laughing at my friend that I collided with a pool stick. The man holding the stick was bent over, obviously preparing to take a shot. When the two of us collided he scratched. The other man standing at the table clapped.

"Damn," he said, shaking his head.

"Sorry," I said, stepping back.

"No, it's my bad," he said, standing up straight before turning around to face me. It was my A-Ex driver! He stared at me for a brief second, then asked, "You work at Fashionista. Right?"

"Yes," I said, dryly.

He actually looked nice in his jeans and baby-blue, button-down shirt. If he wasn't such an asshole, I probably would have considered him handsome. Unfortunately, his rudeness with me at work was a turnoff.

"I thought so," he said. He stood with both hands on top of his pool stick, looking at me like we were on friendly terms and he was expecting a conversation.

"Excuse me," I said. I waited for him to move before walking off.

"Who was that?" LaShay questioned, as soon as I reached the table.

"My A-Ex man," I said, taking a sip of my drink before sitting down.

"He's fine," she said, looking in his direction. "What's his name?"

"Jerk," I replied. I glanced in the man's direction and saw that he was watching me. I frowned before looking away.

LaShay stared at me from across the table. "Why you call him that?" She questioned. I brought both of them up to speed on my previous run-ins with the man.

"Maybe you intimidate him," Anitra said.

"How?" I asked.

"You know some men find women in authority threatening," Anitra said, shrugging her shoulders.

"Yeah, stupid ones," I said.

"Insecure ones," Anitra said.

"Broke ones," I added.

"The ones with little dicks." LaShay jumped in.

The three of us erupted in laughter. "Although I don't think your friend has that problem," LaShay added. She licked her lips while raising her eyebrows. "Looks like he's working with something." I was so shocked by her bluntness, I almost choked on my drink.

"I could care less," I said, wiping my lips. "But how can you tell?"

"Look at how he's standing," she said, nodding in his direction. "I bet he's working with a monster."

I casually looked over and saw him standing with his feet shoulder width apart. There was something commanding—regal—about his stance, but that meant nothing when it came down to what was or was not sitting in between his legs.

"He *is* fine," Anitra agreed. Her words were slightly slurred. Anitra had never been much of a drinker. I was surprised she made it through a third of her glass without passing out. "He may be what you need to resolve your sexual issues."

"What issues?" I asked, confused. "I don't have any sexual issues."

"You're not getting any," LaShay said. "That's the issue."

"By choice, ladies," I reminded them. "By choice."

"All work and no play," LaShay said. "Well, you know the rest."

"Leaves you with a lonely coochie and carpal tunnel syndrome," Anitra laughed. LaShay laughed too, before sliding Anitra's glass away from her.

"You have officially reached your limit," LaShay said, shaking her head.

"I'm fine with things just the way they are," I said. I was being honest. I was fine with my decision not to get involved with anyone right now. The truth was, I hadn't so much as brushed shoulders with anyone I felt attracted to. Mainly because the only thing I did was work, go home, and then work again. "Besides, I'm too busy to commit to anyone right now. The last thing I need is a man complicating things."

I finished my drink, then excused myself from the table. As I walked to the ladies' room I could feel eyes penetrating me. I looked up and found him staring at me again. When I felt a tingle in my clit, I turned my head quickly. Must be the alcohol, I thought to myself.

After handling my business in the ladies' room, I stepped back onto the floor of the pool hall only to find LaShay and Anitra were no longer at the table where I had left them.

"Over here, Toi," I heard LaShay call.

I quickly scanned the room and spotted her and Anitra occupying a table directly beside the one where the A-Ex guy had been playing when I bumped into him. LaShay and Anitra weren't alone; he and the man he had been playing with stood by the table engaging my friends in conversation. I frowned, then exhaled slowly while approaching the table.

"What was wrong with our previous choice of seating?" I asked. I sat on the empty chair opposite Anitra, which happened to be closest to where *he* was standing.

"It was too crowded back there," LaShay said mischievously. "Plus, we saw these two fine gentlemen all alone and we decided, who better to keep them company than the three of us?" She winked at me, then turned to the man standing beside her. He was attractive, short with dark skin, a bald head, and light-brown eyes. He wore a white button-down shirt and dark jeans. It was obvious he and Mr. A-Ex were related. There were several similarities in their facial features.

"Toi, this is Robert," LaShay said, looking from me to the man. "Robert, this is Toi."

"What's up," Robert said, directing his attention to me momentarily.

"Hi." I smiled politely.

"And this is Carlton," LaShay said excitedly. She nodded in Mr. A-Ex's direction. "Carlton, this is Toi."

"It's nice to meet you again, Toi," Carlton said, looking at me.

"When did you introduce yourself the first time?" I asked, staring at him. I smiled sweetly but my voice oozed with sarcasm. I heard LaShay clear her throat while Anitra made a frail, drunken attempt to kick me underneath the table. She missed. I looked from Anitra to LaShay, silently telling them to knock it off. I was going to speak my mind. Besides, as I was outside of work, I had a perfect opportunity to let Carlton know exactly how I felt about his attitude.

"I guess I deserve that," he said.

"No need to guess," I said with my eyebrows raised. "You

do."

He lowered his eyes while looking at me. There was something seductive and dangerous behind his stare. Something that was causing my nipples to grow harder with every second. I crossed my arms across my chest in an attempt to hide my personal peep show, while reminding myself that I didn't like his ass.

"You're right," he agreed. "I do and I'm sorry."

I remained silent for a brief moment. I was shocked that he had given in so quickly. I expected our banter to continue at least for a third round. Maybe he did find me intimidating.

"Apology accepted," I finally said.

He smiled brightly, revealing a dimple in each of his cheeks. I wondered why I hadn't noticed them before, then reminded myself I had never seen the man smile. I admired him silently for a moment before finally looking away.

"Carlton, Toi is a wonderful pool player," LaShay said, looking at me with a mischievous grin on her face.

"Really now?" Carlton asked, sounding intrigued. "How good?"

"Good enough to know how *not* to scratch," I teased, looking at him again.

"Oh, so you got jokes," he laughed lightly.

"I'm just saying," I said innocently.

"Are you challenging me to a game?" he asked.

"Are you accepting?"

"Go get a stick," he said.

"We hope she gets yours," Anitra whispered. I spun around, staring at her with my eyes wide.

"It's the alcohol," she said, holding up a finger. "My bad."

I rolled my eyes at her, then looked back at Carlton. "Game on," I said.

# Chapter 6

## Lisa

After I dialed 911, two uniformed officers came to our home and questioned Carlton and me. Carlton's story was that I started our little quarrel, and that he grabbed me as a snap reaction to my punching him in the face. I attempted to explain my side of the story but I couldn't, due to the waterfall of tears that continued to flow from my eyes. However, I did manage to choke out that Carlton grabbed me and slammed me against the door in front of our son. I also stated that I was only attempting to prevent his departure out of fear that he would take away our son. I may have gotten the details of the argument out of sequence, and I may have misconstrued a few things for my benefit; however, in the end I was the one with the bruises. That meant Carlton was the one going to jail. Ultimately they only held him for 12 hours, which I assumed would be long enough for him to come to his senses and realize the error of his ways.

I was wrong. When I came home from work the next day, I found that Carlton's overnight bag, along with his uniforms and a decent amount of his clothes, were gone. What kind of man just ups and leaves his wife and son without any explanation or warning? Carlton could have had the decency to leave a note but no, he just left us high and dry.

If that wasn't enough, he had the nerve to avoid my phone calls and attempts to make contact. He went for three days without so much as sending me a smoke signal or picking up the phone to say, "Fuck you," until he finally had his cousin Robert accompany him to visit CJ. I tried to talk to Carlton in private but he refused. In fact, he gave me the silent treatment during his visit. I didn't want Robert to think that I was the problem, so I smiled and played nice the entire time they were over and even offered them something to eat. Before they left, I told Carlton I understood his decision to separate at that moment and apologized if he felt I was wrong for what happened the night of our disagreement.

He responded with a cold dry, "Yeah," then told me he would be in contact before walking out the door.

A week passed and although he called to speak with CJ every day, he still hadn't returned home. I lie in bed staring at the ceiling while running a hand back and forth over the cold cotton sheets. I tossed and turned before finally sitting up against the headboard. Staring at the alarm clock, I watched as the illuminated red digital 10:15 turned to 10:16. I had been lying in bed for an hour unable to sleep. I normally wouldn't turn in so early but with Carlton gone and CJ sleeping there was no one to occupy my time.

Finally, I tossed the covers back and slung my feet over the side off the bed, stepping barefoot onto the carpeted floor. I assumed Carlton was staying at Robert's place, but I couldn't help but wonder what the two of them were up to. The thought of Carlton surrounded by half-naked whores invaded my mind as I walked from the bedroom to the kitchen. Robert probably had hooked him up with three or four classless, tasteless women by now. What if Carlton was with one of them right now? Carlton didn't wear a wedding band because he lost the first one while working. I refused to buy him another one simply out of principle, but now I was thinking I should have. Then again, what difference would it have made? If a woman wants a man, she'll go after him even if he has the word MARRIED tattooed on his forehead! I quickly picked up the phone and dialed his cell number. I counted at least six rings before he finally answered.

"Hello," he answered. The sound of loud music combined with laughter played in the background.

*Is he actually out partying?* I asked myself. I was instantly pissed off at the thought. How could Carlton be out having a good time while I sat at home miserable and lonely? He should be here with me attempting to correct the problems in our marriage, but he was out having a good time instead!

"Did I catch you at a bad time?" I questioned sarcastically.

"Not really," he answered. He spoke loudly.

*Not really?* I repeated to myself.

"Well, what are you doing?" I asked, attempting to remain calm.

The noise in the background slowly began to fade away until I heard what sounded like passing cars. I assumed he had stepped away from the crowd. He finally answered, "Out shooting pool. What's up?"

*What's up?* I thought. *Your wife and son are what's up. That's what's up!*

"I want you to come home so we can talk," I said. "We nee—"

"I think it's best at this time that we spend some time apart," Carlton said, cutting me off.

"We've been apart for a week," I said firmly, pacing back and forth. "How much longer do you want?"

"I don't want to talk about this right now," he said.

"Then when?" I asked, raising my voice.

"I'll let you know when I'm ready," he said coldly.

"No, you need to let me know right now," I snapped. I stopped my pacing and stood firmly in place. "I'm your fucking wife—"

The sound of dead air interrupted my venting. "Hello?" I said loudly in the receiver. "Hello!" He'd hung up on me, pissing me off and making me even more determined to get my point across. I pressed the flash button on the phone and dialed his number again.

"Yeah," he answered loudly.

"Don't *yeah* me!" I yelled. "You're treating me like some random bitch! Carlton, I am your wife!"

He remained silent.

"I cook, clean, and take care of your son and our home. I—"

"You had me arrested, Lisa! Over your bullshit! What kind of woman—better yet *wife*—does that?" he blurted, cutting me off.

"I apologized for that!" I reminded him. "What more do you want me to say or do?"

"Nothing," he said sarcastically. "There's nothing you can do." He hung up again before I could respond. I wasted no time calling him back, but my effort was in vain—my call went straight to voice mail.

I clenched the phone in my hand while attempting to process what Carlton had said. I knew the last thing he wanted was for our marriage to be over, he just needed more time to realize what he had at home and that he needed to get back home to it. Right? Or had I gone too far? I decided not to press the subject with Carlton and instead called my homegirl, Sasha, to talk.

Sasha and I had been friends for nearly ten years. The two of us were inseparable at one time, but marriage and family had put some distance between us. Still, no matter how much or how little we saw or talked to each other, she was the only female I felt I could truly trust.

"Did I catch you at a bad time?" I asked, once she answered the phone.

"Girl, no, I'm just waiting on Shawn to get off work," she said pleasantly. "The two of us are going to the midnight showing of the new Steve Harvey flick."

I was behind on the latest movies and other social events. Lately Carlton and I spent our time at Chuck E. Cheese's or at home, either arguing or just going through the motions. I couldn't remember the last time we'd been out on a date as a couple; hell, I could barely remember the last time we were happy.

"What does he have out?" I asked. I was making conversation because I didn't want to sound selfish for calling only about my problems,

*"Think Like A Man,"* she answered. "It's based on his book, with an all-star cast. It came out two weeks ago but you know I can never get to the theater on opening night. Shawn hates the crowds, and his work schedule is so crazy. Lately he's been working…"

I listened inattentively as Sasha went on and on about her husband and all the great things that were happening for the two of them. She was thrilled: not only had he been promoted to general manager at the car dealership where he worked, but he'd also gifted her with a brand-new car, and they were planning a Caribbean vacation.

"So, what's up with you?" Sasha finally asked. I assumed she finally needed to come up for air.

"Nothing much," I said nonchalantly. After hearing all of her good news, there was no way I was going to share all the crap that was wrong with my own life.

"How is my baby, CJ?" She squealed. "How is Carlton?"

"CJ is fine," I said, smiling proudly. "Sweet as ever."

"And Carlton?" she asked.

"He's great," I lied. "Matter of fact…I should get back to him. I just wanted to call and say hi."

"Oh, okay." She hesitated. "Well, tell him I said hey and kiss CJ for me. Let's try to get together this week. You know I gotta show you my new ride and we need to play catch-up."

*We've caught up enough*. I thought. I was being a hater and less than a friend, but I didn't care. Why did everyone else get to be happy while my shit was all fucked up?

"All right," I said quickly. "Talk to you later."

After the phone call, I sat on the living room sofa sulking. I felt ten times worse than I had before I called her. Things were sugar and spice and just freakin' right for her and I hated it. If misery loves company, hell, I wanted to have a party. I pulled my knees up to my chest as Sasha's words ran through my head. She was happy.

I remembered being that happy and excited reciting every detail about my life with Carlton. I waited four years for Carlton to propose to me. Four years! There were struggles and some issues along the way, mostly because he was involved with another woman at the time. I never met the woman, but from what Carlton described, it wasn't anything serious and they were more like friends with benefits.

However, when I met Carlton the other woman began to express her desire for a commitment. It was too late by that time—I had already slid into Carlton's bed and I was breaking him off properly every night. I know as women we're supposed to be our sister's keeper and all that but the truth was, I couldn't care less about her or her emotions. Hell, if she knew how to play her cards right she would have solidified her place as his wife. She didn't know what she had until it was too late, but me? I knew Carlton was a winner at first sight and I was willing to do anything, and I do mean anything, to get him because I knew he was worth it. Not only was he educated, but he was one of the hardest-working men I've ever known.

When we first met, I had a full-time job working at a local restaurant, barely making ends meet. However, after we'd made a commitment, Carlton allowed me to quit working. All I had to do was give him sex how and when he wanted it, and maintain our home. He was exactly what I'd hoped for, a good-looking man who was capable of providing, and willing to do it. Hell, I worked occasionally now and that was only by choice. I could quit anytime because Carlton was the type who had no problem handling all the bills and taking care of business. Carlton was a provider by nature.

I decided to give talking to my husband one more try, so I dialed his number.

"Yeah," he answered again, loudly. The noise and music were still in the background. I ignored them and my feelings about him being out. I decided to set my pride aside, at least until I got what I wanted: my husband back home.

"Please come home, Carlton," I begged. "Please..."

"Lisa—"

"I need you," I pleaded. I adjusted my tone so that I sounded desperate and needy. I was hoping to play on his sympathy. "Please. I just want to see you. I miss you and I need you. Come over so we can talk—then you can leave. Please." I was wishing and practically holding my breath with the hope that he would agree.

After seconds that felt like hours, he said, "I'm on my way."

Thirty minutes later, I stood admiring my reflection in the bathroom mirror. I looked good despite the fact that I looked as white as a ghost. I made a mental note to make time to go tan as soon as possible. My strawberry-blonde hair hung over my shoulders neatly, while the emerald green satin chemise I wore clung gently to my frame. I ditched the oversized T-shirt and flannel pajama bottoms I wore earlier for a nightie that stopped just above my knees. I planned to capture my husband's attention in more ways than one. It had been a while since the two of us had had sex—a month to be exact—and I was hoping, nope, I was counting on Carlton being tipsy and yes, horny.

I checked in on CJ and saw that he was still fast asleep in his bed, then went to wait for Carlton in our bedroom. I sat on the edge of our king-size bed with my freshly shaven legs crossed. I had touched up every area on my body in anticipation of Carlton's visit. I knew I had screwed up by calling the police and ultimately getting on my husband's bad side; now I had to pull a few tricks out my bag to smooth things over. Hell, it wouldn't be the first time I had to do a little damage control.

A year ago, I'd gotten caught up in a little fling with a man named Lance. Lance was a dark-skinned, good-looking brother with a bald head, medium build, and dark brown eyes with long, black, curly lashes that make him look somewhat like a baby doll. The two of us met at Knology Cable, where I worked in customer service and he worked in installations.

Our fling started at the company's annual holiday party. I had chosen to go to the event alone because Carlton had pissed me off. He had chosen to help his sister, Charlotte, move into her new home. I had no problem with him helping his sister, but I didn't appreciate that he chose to do so the day that I had something planned for us—even if I didn't make the decision to go until the night before. I didn't and I still don't feel that I need to make an advance appointment with my husband when I want him to accompany me somewhere. I felt he should have canceled whatever commitment he made to his sister and dedicated that time to getting prepared to escort me to the party. I'll give him credit, he finished helping Charlotte an hour or so before the party was scheduled to start, but by that time I was not in the mood to deal with him.

So I went solo and ended up having a good time—too good a time—without him. At the party I mixed, mingled, and had a few drinks. Lance was also there and as usual, he was looking good and doing some heavy flirting. It wasn't the first time he had come on to me, but that night was the first time I actually responded. I liked the attention I was getting and again, he was looking good.

After a couple of hours of flirting and a few more drinks, he invited me back to his house to hang out. My first thought was to say no and go home to my husband and son. That was until I called to check on CJ, and Carlton started complaining about the attitude I'd given him before I left. His comments spun into an argument that ended with my telling him I was going out with some of the girls from the office and advising him not to wait up.

I accepted Lance's offer and followed him back to his apartment. It was not my original intent to sleep with him. I just wanted his company. When we first arrived at his place, Lance said he could tell something was on my mind. I told him about my problems at home and about my argument with Carlton. He listened and made me laugh until one thing led to another and we ended up screwing on his living room sofa.

Our affair went on for a month until his girlfriend, Brooke, found out about us. Brooke used the typical female method to find out about me: she went through his phone and saw my texts as well as pictures I had sent him, many of which were X-rated. She not only came to our job to confront me, but she went through the trouble of calling my home and speaking with Carlton. I still kick myself for using our landline. When Carlton confronted me with the information I was at a loss for words and caught red-handed. He was hurt and angry, and I thought he was going to walk out, but he never did. He did however warn me that the next time I violated, it would be the end. After that incident I quit my job at Knology, and began helping my Aunt Ellen from time to time in her hair salon.

I stared at the alarm clock on the nightstand. It was now 11:00 pm. What is taking him so damn long? I asked myself. I thought about picking up the phone and calling him again but decided to be patient. If my husband said he was coming, he would come. He would never leave me waiting. I slid back on the bed against the headboard then yawned lightly. I closed my eyes, deciding to take a quick nap until Carlton arrived.

# Chapter 7

## Toi

Denny's had a small crowd, but there wasn't more than a 20-minute wait for food. LaShay and I sat side by side at a table near the kitchen, Carlton sat opposite me, while Robert occupied the chair directly across from LaShay. After Carlton beat me in not one but three games of pool, we decided to grab something to eat. Actually, LaShay decided she wanted breakfast and insisted that the rest of us join her. Kelvin picked up Anitra shortly after Carlton and I started our game, which left just the four of us.

I was making serious headway with the small stack of pancakes in front of me while listening to LaShay and Robert discuss relationships in between bites of their own food. Carlton was also quiet as he devoured his omelet.

Earlier the two of us laughed and joked while we played pool, and shared some information about ourselves. I learned that his last name was Thomas, he was thirty-three, lived in Madison, Alabama, enjoyed playing basketball, and was a movie buff. He'd also told me that he graduated from Strayer University with a bachelor's degree in Business. He always planned to open his own business, but got so caught up with working and trying to make a living that he kept putting the dream on the back burner. After his son, Carlton Jr., was born, his desire to be a provider killed the dream.

Out of sheer curiosity I asked him about his son's mother and he explained it was a crazy and complicated story. He chose not to elaborate and I didn't ask him to. He told me his parents lived in and were originally from Birmingham, Alabama, and that he had an older sister, Charlotte, who once lived in Huntsville but recently relocated to Birmingham to be closer to their parents. I told him I was an only child and that my parents, Diana and Anthony, were Huntsville natives now living in Houston, Texas. I also shared with him my plans to someday return to school and get my degree.

I finished off my pancakes, then patted my stomach.

"Was it good?" Carlton asked, looking at me.

"Delicious," I said. "Either that or I was extremely hungry."

"Probably a little of both," he suggested.

I nodded my head in agreement.

"How was your omelet?" I asked, wiping the corners of mouth with my napkin.

"I've had better," he said. "Usually the ones I make."

"Oh, so you not only beat ladies in pool but you can cook?" I asked, with raised eyebrows. I was slightly salty that he had beaten me and it was my nonchalant way of letting him know.

"Yes," he laughed. "I can cook. One of the many things my mother taught me."

"Impressive," I said, sincerely.

"She also taught me that women like you would find it offensive for a man to let them win simply because they are women."

"Women like me?" I asked. "What kind of woman do you

think I am?"

"Strong-willed," he said. "Intelligent."

"So who taught you how to spit that game?" I asked, teasing.

"It's true, I can tell you're all that and more," he said seriously. "Besides, I don't have any game. I think you know that by now." The way he stared into my eyes made me feel like he was staring through to my soul, and caused my clit to throb almost unbearably.

"You've definitely got something," I said lowly, while squeezing my thighs together.

His lips spread into a sexy smile that only further excited me. I could see LaShay staring at me out of the corner of my eye. I pulled my gaze from Carlton and acknowledged my friend.

"I think we better get going," she said, with raised eyebrows. "It's past my bedtime."

"Yeah, mine too." I said, standing.

"Are you working tomorrow?" Carlton asked, standing also.

"No, I'm off, but I always bring paperwork home," I said. "I work even when I'm off."

"Toi, you and Carlton go ahead," LaShay said. "Robert and I will handle the check."

"Oh, you're treating?" I asked, surprised.

"Umm hum, you know I got this," she said, winking.

I knew what she meant was that Robert "had it" and he was going to pay. LaShay was a moneymaker, but there was no way she'd ever spend her own money if there was a man she could get to spend his. I also knew that despite her entertaining Robert all night, there was no chance of them hooking up after he let it drop that he had five kids by two different women. That put him out of the game. LaShay confirmed this when she casually turned to me and gave me the hand signal meaning "cutthroat."

I grabbed my bag and led the way out the restaurant and toward my car. Although it was the end of April, the late-night air felt more like late October; it was slightly chilly. I ran my hands across my arms in an attempt to soothe the goose bumps that had instantly appeared. I unlocked my car doors, dropped my bag on the passenger's seat, then stood by the driver's side waiting for LaShay and Robert to exit the restaurant. Carlton stood beside me looking up at the sky.

"What's on your mind?" I asked.

"Nothing," he said, looking over at me. "Just thinking about how nice tonight was."

"It was," I agreed.

"Yes, no drama, just a good time," he said. "With good company." He paused, then smiled, once again showing off his straight teeth and dimples. I blushed slightly.

"You really should smile more often," I suggested.

"Really?" he asked. "Why is that?"

"Because smiling is sexy," I said softly.

"So, is that your secret?" he asked, leaning slightly toward me.

My heart rate slowly began to increase as I looked at him. I wasn't sure if it was the alcohol I had consumed or the fact that I had been in heat for nearly two years, but practically every word that fell out of his mouth was causing me to act like a sex-deprived sixteen-year-old girl! I looked past him and saw LaShay and Robert coming toward us. The two of them walked with their arms interlocked.

"Well, it was fun," LaShay said, hugging me. "Call me to let me know you made it in."

"I will," I said, giving her a tight squeeze.

"Nice meeting you." Robert smiled.

"You too," I said pleasantly. I watched as the two of them

walked off in the direction of LaShay's car.

"I guess I'll see you at work," I said slowly, while reaching for my door handle.

"I'll be there," Carlton answered. "Let me get that."

I stepped back, allowing him to open the door for me, then climbed in. "Thank you," I said appreciatively.

"You're welcome." He flashed his dimples at me one last time, then shut the door. I started the engine, then rolled down the window.

"Be safe," he said. He paused for a moment, then turned in the opposite direction. I watched him as he walked away, asking myself why I didn't at least get his number or see if he had plans for the weekend. Because, I said to myself, I don't do that. I'm not the aggressor; men are supposed to approach me. I give them a little bait and they're supposed to jump for it. Besides, what if things went wrong? We'd still have to look at each other at work. I was attempting to reason with myself. I finally concluded that I had a million and one reasons not to stop Carlton but I stopped him anyway. "Carlton," I called out the window.

# Chapter 8

## Lisa

I woke up to the sounds of birds chirping lightly outside my bedroom window and CJ pulling an eyelid up with his tiny fingers. He stood by the bed wearing nothing but his pajama bottoms and socks. The first thing my son did every morning when he woke up was take off his shirt. He'd had this habit since he was two. I had no clue who or where he got the habit from but it was cute. I smiled at him, then took his hand and pressed it to my lips.

"Eggs," he said, scratching his head.

I smiled, then yawned. "Good morning," I said.

"Good morning Mommy," he said. "Eggs."

"Let Mommy take a shower, then I'll fix your eggs." I laughed.

"Eggs," he repeated once more, before turning and scurrying away.

I looked at the alarm clock sitting on the nightstand and saw that it was seven o'clock. I was so caught up in my son's morning entertainment that it took me a minute to realize Carlton was not lying next to me. I climbed out of bed and immediately began checking the entire house, including our spare bedroom. Once I came to the conclusion that he hadn't come home at all, I was not only pissed but concerned as well.

I took a quick shower, then fixed CJ his plate of eggs as thoughts of worry ran rampant through my head. Had something happened to him? Did he get caught up in some bullshit while out with Robert? What? I picked up the phone then dialed his cell. I immediately got his voice mail. I tried again, only to receive his voice mail again.

"What the hell," I said aloud.

"What the hell," CJ repeated as he sat in the living room in front of the television, watching cartoons and eating his eggs. I normally would correct him about repeating what I said, but at the moment at the moment I wasn't in the mood. I tried Carlton's cell one last time before finally deciding to call Robert's home. I sat down at the kitchen table, then dialed the number.

"Yo," he answered, sounding slightly sleepy.

"Hey Robert, it's Lisa," I said pleasantly. "How you doing?"

"Hold on." He exhaled loudly. Rude ass, I thought to myself. A second later I heard what sounded like a door opening and him calling Carlton. It's good to know he's alive, I thought. My concern had turned to sarcasm.

"Yo C," he yelled. "C! Telephone, man…Telephone! It's Lisa. Yeah…"

I heard someone pick up on the line then Carlton yelled, "I got it." I waited until I heard the click confirming that Robert had hung up.

"Hello." Carlton's voice was low and deep. It was obvious I had wakened him too.

"Why aren't you answering your phone?" I questioned immediately.

"My battery died."

"I thought you were coming over last night," I said, calmly.

"I was," he yawned. "But I got caught up in another game."

"Oh," I said, sarcastically. "So you lied to me for what reason?"

*Silence.*

"Hello?" I asked.

"First of all, it wasn't my intent to lie but I got caught up..."

"Intentions don't matter, Carlton," I said. "Actions do."

"Remember that," he said, clearing his throat.

I could feel my blood boiling but I didn't want to explode. The two of us were already sleeping in two different homes; the last thing I wanted was to drive the wedge further between us.

"You could have called," I said, swallowing my pride. "I woke up this morning and got worried."

"I told you my battery died," he said, clearing his throat. "And what are you worried for now? You weren't worried when I spent the night in jail."

"I said I was sorry about that," I grunted. "Damn, how long are you going to hold that against me?"

"I'm not holding anything against you," he said. "I'm just reminding you of how we got here."

I didn't need a reminder of anything! I was well aware of what was said and done.

"I'm quite aware of what got us here," I advised him. "I'm trying, Carlton—"

"Okay," he said, snickering slightly. "If you say so."

"What the hell do you want me to do?"

"What the hell," CJ repeated.

"CJ!" I snapped, cutting my eyes at him. "Stop repeating everything you hear!"

"Don't yell at him," Carlton commanded. "It's not his fault you don't know how to talk in front of him. You need to learn."

"Don't tell me what I need to learn! Mother—"

"Put my son on the phone," he ordered, cutting me off.

"If you want to speak to your son," I said loudly. "You'll bring your ass home!" I hung up before he could respond.

"Whew!" I screamed, slamming the phone down on the table. I shook my head while thinking about the conversation. Why was he acting like this? I was willing to do what I needed to do to smooth things over with my husband, but I was not going to allow him to keep throwing shit up in my face.

"Mommy," CJ called.

I looked up and saw him staring at me with his beautiful, big brown eyes and immediately felt like dirt. I had gotten caught up in my conversation with Carlton and taken my frustration out on my son. That was something I tried never to do.

"Yes, baby?" I asked, smiling slowly.

"I want to talk to Daddy," he said innocently. He stared at me, then quickly returned his attention back to the TV. I pondered over CJ's words, then exhaled loudly. I thought to myself that sometimes it takes the voice of a child to extinguish our inner storms, as I dialed Carlton's number. This time the phone rung and he answered on the third ring.

"Yeah," he said. I could tell he had his defenses up and if I was willing, he would argue with me. I decided to get straight to the point.

"CJ wants to speak with you," I said solemnly.

I rose from the table and walked over and handed CJ the phone. "Telephone baby, it's Daddy." I eased down on the couch while listening to CJ gab with his father about his cartoons and what he had for breakfast. I was hoping that my calling Carlton back would show him some initiative on my behalf, and that he would now speak to me without his previous and obvious resentment. However, when CJ said, "Love you too…Bye-bye," then put down the phone it was clear that I was hoping on a lost cause. I excused myself to my bedroom, slamming the door behind me.

# Chapter 9

## Toi

After getting home late I decided I would sleep in, but my plan was foiled when LaShay called, waking me up the next morning. I wondered what she wanted, considering we had spent an hour on the phone discussing the evening's events after I called to let her know I was safely home.

"Good morning!" she piped up from the other end of the phone.

"Good morning," I said, stretching my legs.

"So, what time is your date with Carlton?" she inquired.

She was referring to the fact that, when I called Carlton back to my car, I gave him my number and made tentative plans to see him later in the day.

"I don't know," I said honestly. "I haven't spoken with him yet."

"Who makes a date without scheduling a time?"

"A tentative date," I corrected her. "And who calls at…What time is it?"

"1:30," she informed me.

"What?" I asked. I sat straight up in the bed and looked at the alarm clock sitting on my nightstand. She was right. I guess

I *had* slept in.

"You heard me," she said.

"I can't believe I slept this late," I grumbled.

"It's probably long overdue," LaShay said. "Anywho, so what time are we going shopping?"

"We're not," I said.

The last place I wanted to be on a Saturday was at a mall with LaShay. I loved to shop like every other woman I know but with LaShay, a 30-minute trip to the mall always turned into a three-hour ordeal.

"So what are you going to wear?" she questioned.

"Wear when?"

"On your date tonight!" she said loudly.

"I don't know." I yawned again. "I'll find something in my closet."

"Umm…"

"Umm, what?"

"I've seen your closet and your date wardrobe hasn't been updated since Justin." She said.

LaShay was right. I had bought plenty of new clothes for work but nothing glam enough for an after-hours event. I suddenly felt self-conscious about my attire.

"Well, first I need to know where and *if* we're going, then—" I paused when I heard my call waiting beep. "Hold on," I said.

"Hello?" I answered the other line.

"Hi Toi, it's me, Carlton."

"Hey," I said, trying to suppress a smile.

"Did I catch you at a bad time?"

"Not at all."

"Great," he said. "I was thinking the two of us could have dinner together. That is, if you're still free?"

*Am I free?* I thought. *You have no idea.* "Yes, we can," I said.

Cool," he said. "Do you like seafood?"

"Love it."

"Great. There's this little spot by the lake in Guntersville, I want to take you there," he informed me. Guntersville was at least 50 minutes from Huntsville. I wondered why he wanted to go so far out for seafood. I decided not to question the location and just go with the flow.

"Sounds good," I said happily.

"How is 7:30?"

"7:30 is fine," I said, tossing back the covers. If I planned to find something to wear, I knew I had to get moving. I eased out of bed while giving him my address. Then I realized I had forgotten all about LaShay on the other end.

"Hello," I said, clicking back over.

"That was him," she concluded. "Wasn't it?"

"Yes."

"Where are you two going?"

"Dinner at 7:30," I said, walking toward my bathroom.

"So, am I driving to the mall or are you?"

"I'll be by to pick you up in an hour."

*****

LaShay and I ventured out to Parkway Place Mall in search of the perfect dress. After an hour and ten dresses later, she helped me pick out a sexy but mature, curve-fitting, above-the-knee lace dress that I loved. I found a pair of red, five-inch, animal-print platform heels to complete my look and I was set. Before I dropped LaShay off at home, she gave me a keen warning to loosen up and try to have a good time without overanalyzing

Carlton's every move.

"I won't over analyze," I said. "I never do."

She gave me a blank stare before continuing. "Also try to step outside your box," she said. "Don't be so technical and by the book."

"What are you talking about?" I asked.

"I don't kiss on the first date," she said, mimicking me. "No holding hands." She waved her hand in the air, then shook her head. "All that extra."

"Get out," I said, unlocking the car doors.

"I'm just saying," she laughed. "Oh, I got something for you."

I watched as she dug inside her handbag, eventually pulling out several boxes of condoms.

"I got you the average and the Magnums," she said. "If I'm right you won't be using the average." She looked at me, smiling.

"Shay? Really?"

"What?" she asked, with raised eyebrows.

"I don't need condoms," I said, shaking my head.

"What you got some?" she questioned.

"I don't need any," I advised her. I planned to have a good time but not *that* good of a time.

"You never know," she said, holding her hand out to me. "It's better to be safe than crying."

*****

Carlton knocked on my door at exactly 7:30 pm. I did a quick scan over my apartment to make sure everything was in place before approaching the door. I opened it and found Carlton there, holding three long-stemmed yellow roses and looking so good I did a double take. He wore khakis and a green, button-down Ralph Lauren shirt. His eyes lit up at the sight of me as I'm sure mine did at the sight of him.

"Hey, beautiful." He smiled and handed me the roses. "You look, well, beautiful."

"Thank you," I smiled. "You look handsome."

He grinned in return. "Are you ready?" he asked, extending his hand to me. I hesitated only for a second, then slipped my hand in his.

"Ready," I said, while silently admiring the warmth and softness of his skin.

Carlton and I walked hand and hand as he escorted me down the sidewalk toward the parking lot, to a black Chrysler 300 with dark, tinted windows. The paint shone under the moonlight like diamonds. He held the door open for me before walking around to the driver's side.

"Nice car," I said, once he was inside.

"Thank you."

I relaxed against the cool leather seat while enjoying the sound of Ne-Yo belting "Lazy Love" from the stereo speakers. So far Carlton was batting a thousand. He was on time, came bearing roses, his car was clean inside and out, and he had good taste in music.

"Did you get your paperwork done today?" he asked, as we pulled out of the parking lot.

I had forgotten all about it. "I didn't so much as touch my paperwork today," I admitted.

"Was it because you were so excited to see me?" he asked lightly.

"Actually yes it was," I said, looking over at him.

"That's a good thing," he said, cheesing.

The conversation between us continued to flow freely as

we headed out of the city. We talked about politics, sports, and even the weather. When he eventually asked why I was single, I told him simply that I was focused on being a better me. I had no expectations for us in terms of a relationship. Still, I didn't want to ruin what I felt was going to be a wonderful evening by overloading him with my old relationship baggage.

The restaurant Carlton took me to, Top O' the River, sat directly by Lake Guntersville and had a rustic, cozy feel. There was a large, covered wooden deck outside of the restaurant covered in white lights. When we first walked in, I immediately noticed how courteous and polite the hostess was. I also noted the 50-gallon aquarium with electric-blue lighting and three bright yellow fish swimming inside. The dim, intimate lighting gave the illusion that the fish were directly in front of me. The walls housed framed black-and-white photographs of fishermen with their catch and metal plates identifying different varieties of fish. Just below the pictures were antique-looking fishing rods and reels mounted to the wall.

Our server sat us in the private dining area, which consisted of six booths with leather-covered seats and high wooden backs. On each table there were small metal lanterns with a single tea light burning inside. When our server brought out our dinner, Carlton reached across the table and took both of my hands in his.

"Do you mind?" He asked. "I like to say grace." Impressive! I thought. There was nothing like a praying man!

"Not at all." I grinned, then bowed my head.

During dinner the two of us laughed and conversed as if we had been friends for years. The way we connected almost felt too good and too perfect. After finishing our dinner—stuffed crab and a mixed green salad for me, a rib eye steak and butterfly shrimp for him—Carlton asked for the check. When our server returned, my natural instinct kicked in and I reached for the ticket, preparing to pay.

"None of that," he said, placing his hand on top of the ticket.

"What?" I questioned.

"I appreciate the thought but I got this one," he said, pulling his wallet out his pocket. "And the next one too."

I watched as he pulled out several crisp twenties and dropped them on the table. "That's assuming we have a next time."

"I'd like that," I said, sincerely.

"Good," he said, folding his hands together in front of him. "So, what are you doing tomorrow?"

I had planned to relax in nothing but my favorite pair of boy shorts and tank top. No makeup. No curlers. Just me in all my natural glory, doing positively nothing. However, it was evident those plans were changing. "I don't know," I said, shrugging my shoulders. "What do you want to do?" I asked sweetly.

"Some partners of mine are having a cookout," he said. "I would like it if you come with me."

"Sounds like a plan."

"Good," he smiled back. "Come on." He stood, then reached for my hand. "I want to show you something before we leave."

I took his hand and allowed him to assist me out the booth. Carlton led me out one of the restaurant's side doors and down a small, pebble-covered trail until we reached a long, wooden dock. He held my hand tightly as we strolled underneath the light of the glowing moon and twinkling stars. Once we reached the end of the dock, we stood with our fingers entwined, staring out at the dark waters.

"You know, I noticed you the very first day I saw you," he confessed.

"Beyond that stank attitude of yours?" I teased. "Really?"

"Yes, beyond my attitude," he laughed. "I still haven't made up for that one yet. Huh?"

"Nope," I joked.

"How can I redeem myself?" he asked, turning to face me.

"I don't know," I said, shaking my head. "I mean you're off to a good start but—"

My words and my thoughts were cut short when he pressed his lips to mine, silencing me with a kiss. There was a time when I would never allow a man to kiss me on the first date. That time was long gone. I slid my hand up to Carlton's neck and kissed him as if I had never kissed a man before. He pulled me closer, wrapping his arms around me while our tongues touched, rubbed, and did all the things at that moment that I secretly wished we were doing with our bodies. When he attempted to pull away I pulled him closer. By the time we came up for air, my panties were soaking and there was a very noticeable bulge pushing against his pants. He looked at me and smiled.

"Damn," he said, easing away from me slowly. He turned away from me, untucked his shirt from inside his pants, then faced me again. I thought it was cute and sexy how he went above and beyond to be a gentleman. The truth was, the only thing I was thinking about at that second was his standing in front of me naked as the day he was born.

"I know," I said, slowing my breathing. "Damn is right."

My heart was beating fiercely in my chest, while my body felt like there were a trillion butterflies flapping their wings inside.

*****

We drove back to Huntsville in silence. I smiled while staring out the window, watching the streetlights as they passed and faded into the darkness. It felt good to be in a man's company again. I confessed, I truly missed kissing and being held. When John Legend's "Tonight" came on, Carlton cranked the volume up slightly, then reached over and caressed my hand. His touch sent a sensation like a shot through my fingers to my veins. I looked over at him and admired the cut of his jaw and the sculpting of his lips. As I listened to John crooning, "I don't wanna brag but I'll be the best you ever had," the only thing I could think about was reliving my sexual frustration. I stretched my legs out in front of me, then took Carlton's hand and placed it on my thigh. He pulled his eyes away from the road ahead briefly and looked at me. I smiled seductively. He looked back to the road while slowly rubbing and stroking my thigh. I had nonverbally given him permission to explore further but he stayed in what I like to call the safe zone: mid-thigh to knee, no more, no less. I was once again impressed with his behavior and self-control. However, my hot box felt like it was going to jump from under my dress! Now, I knew I was breaking every rule in those self-help, how-not-to be-labeled-as-a-hoe books that were flooding the country—as well as my own personal rules—but I was following my natural instincts with Carlton and again, I felt comfortable with him. So comfortable that when we made it back to my apartment, I invited him in.

"Would you like something to drink?" I asked, clutching my keys and bag in my hand. "Water…coffee…soda…?" *Me?* I thought to myself.

"No, I'm fine. Thank you," he said, walking over to my sofa and sitting down. I looked at him and observed that he looked as nervous as I felt. Maybe this was a bad idea, I thought to myself. What was I thinking? The problem was I *wasn't* thinking, I was caught up in some spur-of-the-moment nonsense and now I was having regrets. I stood by my front door, engulfed in my thoughts and feeling like a fool.

"Come here, please," he asked, breaking my trance.

I did as he requested, dropping the items in my hand on the coffee table. I eased down beside him on the sofa while looking in his eyes. If hunger had a stare, I imagine it would emulate Carlton's gaze. If hot-in-the-ass had a poster child, I would have been the model because in zero to sixty seconds I was all over him. I pushed him back against the sofa, kissing him hard on the lips. Carlton's hands moved from my hips to my back until finally, he buried his fingers in my hair. I pulled my lips from his, then kissed him from his neck up to his ear. I licked then sucked his earlobe while cupping the back of his head.

"Toi," he breathed deeply. "Toi, wait."

Wait? I asked myself. I pulled back and looked at him.

"What's wrong?" I asked, attempting to catch my breath.

"Nothing's wrong," he said, stroking my cheek with his fingertips. "But if you keep doing that…if we keep going…I can't guarantee you I'm going to be able to restrain myself. So, unless you want me to keep going…we'd better stop. I'm a patient man…I'm willing to wait."

I sat back on the sofa while processing his words and trying to get a handle on my own thoughts. I took a deep breath, then exhaled slowly through my parted lips. I was truly impressed with how chivalrous he was being, but I was also extremely horny. I stared at him, then took a long, cleansing breath.

"Okay," I said, agreeing with him. He stood, then pulled me up and into his arms. He gave me a hug and kissed my cheek.

"So I'll see you tomorrow?" he asked, looking at me.

"Yes, "I smiled. "Are you available for breakfast in the

morning?"

"Yes, I am," he said.

"Good," I said. "You can tell me what you like in the morning." I took him by the hand, leading him to my bedroom.

*****

I would love to tell you that Carlton was the best I ever had; unfortunately, he was a no- go. First, let me give him his props, he was definitely working with something: he didn't have what I consider a monster but he was still slightly above average. He took his time kissing me and although he didn't go down, I was still optimistic about things to come. However, that all changed when his man wouldn't stay up long enough to put on the condom. I even tried giving him a hand job; it just wasn't moving!

"I'm sorry," he said, shaking his head. He sat on the edge of the bed with his back to me.

"It's okay," I said, nicely. It *wasn't*, but what else was I going to say? Besides, I still liked spending time with him, so he still had a few points scored with me.

"Do you want me to go?" he asked.

"No," I said, frowning. "Why?"

He turned and looked at me with a face that said, *'Why do you think?'*

"No," I said soothingly. "Stay."

He climbed back on the bed, then pulled me into his arms.

"You just keep having to redeem yourself," I teased, trying to lighten his mood.

"I know." He blew. "I know."

I settled into the comfort of his arms, then closed my eyes and drifted off to sleep.

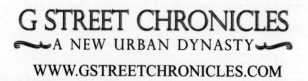

# Chapter 10

## Lisa

I had stretched out across my bed with the latest issue of *People* magazine spread in front of me when I heard the front door open. I immediately jumped off the bed, worried that CJ, whom I'd left playing in the living room, had opened the door. When I heard him squealing, "Daddy!" with excitement I paused.

"Daddy!" he said again, joyously.

"Hey man," I heard Carlton say. "What you doing?"

"Playing," CJ replied.

I quickly went to the bathroom. I brushed my hair down and smoothed my hands over the front of my tank top and shorts. I wasn't wearing makeup, which was fine; Carlton preferred me all natural.

I joined my husband and son in the living room. Carlton was a sight for sore eyes in a burnt-orange T-shirt and denim shorts. His skin seemed to glow underneath the light in the room. He sat on the floor with CJ on his lap. The two of them were rolling one of CJ's matchbox cars across the carpet.

"Hey," I said, leaning against the wall.

"Hey," Carlton said.

There was no enthusiasm in his voice and he didn't even bother looking up at me. I took a deep breath, then exhaled slowly through my parted lips.

"How long are you staying?" I asked, conscious of the tone of my voice. I wanted to be sure that I didn't come off as demanding.

"Not too long," he said. "I just came to spend some time with CJ and see if he needed anything."

"Oh, okay," I said. "We're good, but thank you."

He continued to play with our son while I watched, feeling like a third wheel. I sat down at the kitchen table. *Say something,* I told myself. *Anything.* Where the hell were you last night? Not that.

"Are you hungry?" I asked.

"No, thanks," he said. "I had a big breakfast."

"Did you cook or go out for breakfast?"

He finally raised his head at me. "I went out. Why?"

"I was just asking," I explained quickly. "I'm just making conversation. All right?"

"Yeah."

"Well, I'll let the two of you enjoy your time together," I said, standing. "If you don't mind, can you let me know when you're leaving?"

"Yeah," he said, before refocusing on CJ.

"Thanks."

I returned to my bedroom and my magazine. I was on pins and needles throughout Carlton's visit. After an hour there was a knock on the bedroom door.

"Come in," I said, sitting up.

"Hey, I'm getting ready to dip," he said, standing in the doorway. "I gave CJ some money and told him you would take him to McDonald's later on."

"Thank you for that," I said, rolling my eyes. "Put the pressure on me."

"Yep," he said. "Well, I better get going."

"Okay," I said.

There was an unpleasant silence between us until he finally said, "I'll see you tomorrow."

"Carlton," I blurted, as he turned to leave.

"Yeah?" He asked, turning around to face me again.

"I just want you to know that I'm truly sorry," I said, humbly. "What I did was wrong and I'm sorry. I know that I have been hard to deal with and to be honest I can't blame you for leaving. I have put you through a lot more than most men would be willing to forgive. However, I'm asking you…begging you to please come back home. I need you here, CJ needs you here."

He sighed lowly while shaking his head. "Lisa—"

"No, please just listen," I said, standing. "I'm sorry and I promise if you just come home I will show you how sorry I am and I'll get better…Things will get better…CJ needs his father. You know he does. Please just come home," I begged. "Please."

He looked like he was actually considering my request. I knew if I was going to keep him thinking and get a yes out of him, I needed to make another move. I thought for a moment, hoping the perfect words would come to me. When they didn't I decided to use nonverbal language to express myself. I walked past him and closed the door before turning and pressing my lips to his. Although he didn't pull away, he remained motionless. This was not the reaction I was hoping for. I could remember a time when the only thing I had to do was stand in front of Carlton and he would handle the rest.

I was determined to get him to reciprocate. I proved this by kissing him harder on the mouth and forcing his lips apart with my tongue. After a few awkward seconds, which almost pissed me off, I felt the warm-wet touch of his tongue connecting with mine, and his warm breath. I was slightly breathless when I pulled away.

"Please come home," I pleaded, staring into his dark brown eyes.

He looked away then shook his head. "It's not that simple Lisa," he said. "It's obvious that we have some major issues and I don't—"

I kissed him again, preventing him from completing his sentence. I didn't want to hear anything but yes and if Carlton wasn't ready to say that word to me, then it was evident that I needed to do a lot more persuading. While I continued to seduce his tongue with mine, I reached down and grabbed his belt. In less than sixty seconds I had my husband's boxers and pants down around his ankles and I was kneeling before him. I wrapped my lips around his limp dick and began sucking it like my life depended on it. I bobbed my head back and forth until every inch of Carlton was covered and damn near dripping in my saliva. I held his man steady with one hand while massaging his nuts with the other. I looked up at Carlton and felt sheer delight as I observed the expression of pleasure etched in his face. I was hitting Carlton below the belt and it was working.

I licked and sucked gently until he was rock hard and pushing in and out in between my lips. Grabbing the back of my head with both hands, he rotated his torso, grinding inside my mouth. He went deeper with every rotation, forcing me to hold my mouth open and practically gagging me. I placed one hand on each of his thighs in an attempt to regain control. However, Carlton was lost in his own world. I felt the muscles in his thighs tightening as his legs began to shake lightly. He released his grip on my hair, allowing me to pull away. I dabbed at the corners of my mouth with my fingertips while slowly standing up straight. I stepped backward until I was standing up against the edge of our bed. I lifted my shirt over my head and dropped it to the floor before easing my shorts down and stepping out of them.

I wasn't in the mood earlier but looking at the desire in Carlton's eyes quickly changed that; I could feel myself getting wetter by the second. I climbed on the bed, then lay on my back with my legs spread wide. I continued to watch Carlton as he stood looking at me. He hesitated for a moment, then finally removed what clothes he still had on and made his way over to the bed.

It was a good thing for me that I was aroused because he didn't bother with foreplay or so much as offering my lower lips any special attention. Instead he climbed on top of me and immediately pushed himself inside. Carlton is normally slow and gentle with his lovemaking but today was different. He beat me from the inside quickly. I assumed he was taking his sexual and emotional frustration out on me the only way he knew how. I flinched, slightly from the pleasure and the pain that he was providing but found no reason to complain. He pushed my legs back until my knees were up by my ears, diving deeper with each and every stroke. I ran my hand across the soft hairs on his chest while staring into his eyes. Carlton's breathing was heavy and rugged as he pushed in and out, over and over.

"Ohhh," I moaned loudly. I could feel myself on the verge of an orgasm. When Carlton let out a deep grunt I knew he was too and I didn't want him beating me to the finish line.

"Slow down," I moaned. "Slow down..."

He ignored my request and five seconds later his body

stiffened as he came inside of me, then collapsed on the bed next to me. Although my husband hadn't allowed me time to have my own orgasm, I was content and convinced that he would now come back to me. I watched as he carried his clothes into the bathroom. I slipped my clothes back on, then sat on the edge of the bed waiting for him.

"I'll see you tomorrow," he said, finally exiting the bathroom.

"Where are you going now?" I asked.

"Back to Robert's," he said casually. I waited for him to continue our conversation. When he didn't, I took the lead.

"You're going back to Robert's to get your clothes?" I assumed.

He ran his hands over the top of his head, then frowned. "No," he said, looking me directly in the eyes. I could hear my answer in his voice before I asked the question.

"So, you're not staying here tonight?" I asked.

"No," he said. He stared at me with a straight face. "I'm not ready yet."

"I just thought," I began. "After what just happened… that…"

The look on Carlton's face was an indication that I had played myself. I nodded my head, then forced myself to smile. "Okay," I said, slowly. "I understand. Call me tomorrow. Maybe we can have dinner or something…"

"Maybe," he said politely before walking past me.

I followed him to the front door. He gave CJ a hug and a kiss before leaving me with my pride on the floor.

# CHAPTER 11

## Toi

The cookout Carlton took me to was held at a beautiful red-brick, two-story home that sat on what had to be at least four acres of land. Surrounded by well-trimmed, vibrant green bushes and well-manicured grass, the home had a country vibe with a touch of elegance. It was located just outside the city limits and if you weren't looking for it, you could quite easily pass by it. Carlton referred to it as "the spot," and advised me the homeowner was a friend of his named Gabe.

"He's somewhat of a flirt," he advised me, as he held open my door. "But he's good people. I've known him for several years. He's like family." He grabbed me by the hand, then smiled.

"Have I told you how good you look?" he asked, staring at me.

"Yes," I laughed. "But let me hear it again."

When I opened the door to my apartment, Carlton had complimented me at least three times on the fitted, blue-striped, halter maxi dress and sandals I had on. I was quite aware that my choice of dress had gained his approval, but I was milking the compliments for all they were worth.

He leaned down and kissed me softly on the lips, then pulled away and smiled.

"Thank you," I said sweetly.

"You're welcome, beautiful."

"And by the way, I'm in good company," I said, admiring the pink Polo shirt and denim shorts he wore.

As we approached the backyard, I could hear the sounds of laughter and music blasting and smell the scent of charcoal. When the two of us came around the corner hand in hand, I saw that there was only one other couple and a single man present. I admired the large deck attached to the back of the home, which housed a built-in hot tub. I was realizing that Gabe had good taste, and if the inside of the home looked anything like the outside, I would have to upgrade that taste from good to excellent.

The couple immediately came up to us and greeted Carlton, while the man continued to stand at the grill. He had his back to us, holding a phone to his ear with one hand while turning steaks over with the other. He was tall with skin the color of toasted almonds.

"Toi, this is Quinton and his lady Nesha," Carlton said, introducing me to the couple. Quinton was handsome: bald, tall, dark-skinned, built, with dark brown eyes and a big smile. Nesha was slim, with a complexion of brown sugar and reddish-blonde micro braids that she wore pulled back in a neat bun. She and Quinton were dressed alike in darkshorts and white T-shirts. Nesha's shirt was cut low, revealing the curve of her breast and a tattoo on her left breast with Quinton's name written in cursive.

"How you doing, Ms. Lady?" Quinton asked, extending his hand to me.

"I'm fine and yourself?" I asked, shaking his hand.

"I'm good," he smiled. He looked at Carlton then said,

"That's what's up." I took his words as approval. It was evident that Carlton did too. He smiled and nodded his head.

"Hey, Toi." Nesha smiled.

"Hello." I smiled in return.

"Listen, we're going to run to the store," Quinton advised us. "What y'all drinking on?"

"Do you drink?" Nesha asked.

"Yes," I admitted.

"What kind of liquor do you like?" she questioned.

"Cognac or vodka," I answered.

"We like that yak," Quinton said.

"Cognac is fine," I said. "Hennessy or Remy."

"Oh shit," he said, nodding his head. "Ms. Lady is a G."

"A win-win," Carlton agreed, removing his wallet from his back pocket.

"No doubt," Quinton laughed. "She's gon' fit right in." Carlton handed him a hundred-dollar bill.

"Get a six pack of Coronas too," he said. "And whatever extra you think of."

"Bet," Quinton said.

"See you in a sec," Nesha said to me.

"Be safe," I said, politely.

"Come on," Carlton said. "Let me introduce you to Gabe." As we approached the man, he ended the call he was on and turned around. Once I got a closer look at him I immediately knew who he was. He was the man I'd run off from selling his merchandise in front of my store. Can this city be any smaller, I asked myself.

"What's up, man," Carlton greeted him.

"Carlton," he said smoothly. "Glad you could make it."

"Toi, this is Gabe," Carlton said, looking from me to the man.

"Gabe, this is Toi."

Gabe smiled and extended his hand to me. When I took it he turned my palm down, then kissed the back of my hand. Gabe wore a gold button-down shirt with khaki shorts and brown sandals. He was a slim man with brown skin and low-cut hair that displayed hints of grey throughout. He looked to be in his early forties, but he had the stance or swagger of a 30-year old. He wasn't an ugly man, but he wasn't what I considered fine either.

"We meet again," he said, staring at me with his dark eyes. "But this time it's in my territory." He gave me a smug grin.

"You two know each other?" Carlton questioned. He looked from Gabe to me.

"This is the lovely young lady who banished me from conducting business in front of her store," Gabe responded before I had the chance. "If I remember correctly, she threatened to call the authorities," he said, clasping his hands together.

"You are correct," I said without shame. "As I remember, you were bad for my sales." I stared at him directly.

"Afraid of competition?" he asked, laughing lightly.

"Afraid of jail?" I asked.

His laughter, along with the cheesy grin plastered on his face, dissolved. His eyebrows inched closer together as his lips formed a frown. I had struck a nerve.

"Should we go?" Carlton asked, slipping his arm around my waist. The gesture was simple, but it made me think he was letting Gabe know he would protect me if need be. I liked the position he was taking, but I was willing to bet money I could hold my own with Gabe. Gabe was a businessman, and from what I had seen of his home so far, a good one. However, his reaction to my mention of jail also gave me the impression he was familiar with the system and he was smart enough to know I wasn't bluffing. Either that or he was crazy enough to try me. One or the other.

Gabe's expression softened. "Now you should know me better than that my friend," he said, slapping his hand on Carlton's shoulder. "This is a place of love and peace. And we're all friends. I was just making a joke, you know I have a sick sense of humor."

"That you do," Carlton agreed.

"So, am I forgiven?" Gabe asked, smiling, then extending his hand to me.

"Sure," I said, with fake sweetness. I shook the man's hand while wondering to myself just how much Carlton trusted him.

"Good," he said. He released my hand slowly, too slowly for my comfort. "Well, why don't the two of you make yourselves at home. The food will be ready shortly."

"Appreciate that," Carlton said, giving his friend a handshake and a brotherly hug.

"Are you sure you're okay?" he asked me, while leading me to the deck. I looked over my shoulder and saw Gabe staring at me.

"Positive," I said, turning my attention to Carlton.

Despite my minor conflict with Gabe, the rest of the evening went by without a hitch. Nesha seemed cool and we talked easily. I even had to give Gabe his props; the meal he prepared was off the chain and he actually turned out to be a great host. Plus, he was courteous and entertaining.

As the sun went down the bugs began to come out in full force. We took shelter inside Gabe's den, where he put one of my favorite Kevin Hart stand-up videos on his big screen. My earlier thought about his taste was confirmed; it was excellent. As I sat between Carlton and Gabe on the suede sectional, I casually admired the setup. From the 52-inch television and home theater system to the suede and wood furnishings, it was obvious that Gabe not only had excellent taste but he was making good money. Dirty money, I'm sure, but good money.

I was feeling slightly lit from the Hennessey and Coke in my cup, and horny from the way Carlton's leg kept rubbing up against mine.

"You better stop," I whispered in his ear suggestively.

"And if I don't ?" he asked.

"You gon' learn today," I teased, mimicking Kevin on the screen. He laughed lowly, then kissed me.

"Carlton, how is Lisa doing?" Gabe asked.

I looked at Carlton, waiting on him to answer Gabe's question. He didn't; instead he looked past me and stared at Gabe strangely. Quinton was laughing at Kevin's jokes, so loudly I was sure Carlton hadn't heard the question.

"He's talking to you," I said.

"I heard him," Carlton replied while staring at Gabe. There was an obvious tension that had just formed between the two men.

"That mutherfucker right there!" Quinton laughed, clapping his hands. "Whew! He a fool!" He continued to stare at the television screen, oblivious to his surroundings. "Y'all hear that shit? Boy, I tell you." He looked at each of us one by one. "What I miss?" he asked, looking at Nesha. She shook her head.

"I was just asking Carlton how Lisa was doing," Gabe told her. "Lisa…" he repeated. He leaned forward on the sofa, then poured another shot of the Patron he had been sipping on.

"Lisa is fine," Carlton said, through almost-clenched teeth. It was obvious Lisa, whoever she may be, was a sore subject for him.

"Who is Lisa?" I asked, curious. Silence. *Don't everyone answer at once*, I thought.

"Toi, I—"

"Lisa is CJ's mother," Gabe answered, cutting Carlton off.

"Oh, your son's mother?" I asked, relieved to have an answer. I remembered Carlton telling me that their history was crazy and complicated. That explained his reaction to Gabe's question.

"Hey, I think it's time for an intermission," Quinton said, easing off the couch. He stood up and adjusted his shirt before pulling out a small bag of weed. "Gabe, you wit' me?"

Gabe looked at Carlton, then nodded his head. He stood then said, "I'm with you, my brother. Carlton, why don't you come get you some contact."

"I'll pass," Carlton said, standing. "It's getting late. Toi and I better get to the other side of town before the boys get out."

"You ready?" Carlton asked me.

"Yes," I said. His mood had lightened slightly, but to me it was obvious that he was still in a funk about Gabe's questions.

"The party's over?" Gabe asked, looking at Carlton. "Come on now. Stay. Shit, I got *three* extra bedrooms. Pick one!" He looked at me, grinning. It was obvious he couldn't hold his liquor.

"We'll pass," Carlton said.

"Pass?" Gabe repeated. "Wow."

"Thanks for the invite," Carlton said.

"You know me," Gabe said, laughing lightly. "Mr. Hospitality."

"Nesha, it was nice meeting you," I said, standing abruptly.

"Umm, you too, girl." She smiled. "I'm going to check out your store as soon as I can."

"Do that," I said smiling.

"Thanks for having us," I said to Gabe. "See you later, Quinton."

"All right, Ms. Lady," Quinton said, giving me a friendly hug. I slipped my hand in Carlton's, then smiled as he led me out the door.

## Chapter 12

# Toi

Carlton wasn't his usual talkative self on the way back to my place and I knew it had to be because of Gabe's questions. How bad could things really be between Carlton and his baby mama? Surely as adults with a child, they had to have a positive line of communication; I would think they would, at least for CJ's benefit. I had several questions about the two of them and the bitterness that seemed to exist between them, but I decided to leave things as they were. I figured when he was ready to open up to me about the drama he would. Besides, I was still floating on an alcohol high and I planned to take full advantage of Carlton. We had unfinished business and I was in the perfect mood to finish it.

I stood at my front door fumbling with my keys with Carlton standing behind me. It was obvious to me that I was a little more buzzed than I thought I was. I was thankful Carlton was designated driver for the night. I finally located my house keys and managed to open the door.

"Whola!" I giggled, once I got the door open.

Once the two of us were inside I plopped down into my leather armchair, immediately kicking off my sandals. Carlton stood in front of the door watching my every move.

"So, are you ready to redeem yourself?" I asked seductively.

He stared at me with something in his eyes that I couldn't quite figure out.

"Toi, I'm married," he said, lowly. He pulled his eyes from mine for a brief second, then looked at me again.

"You're what?" I asked, staring at him.

"I'm married," he repeated. "Lisa is my wife."

I looked at him, waiting for him to laugh or explain somehow that his statement was a joke.

Of course, he never did and truth be told, I knew in my heart he never would. I shook my head while looking at him.

"Perfect," I grumbled. "I said our connection was too good to be true. I was right."

"I know I should have told you before now," he explained. "But it's just that things between us have been moving so smoothly and fast that I got caught up."

"Had you told me you were married, we could have prevented you getting caught up," I said, pissed. I was not only pissed off at him but at myself. Carton didn't tell me he was married and I didn't bother to ask. Hell, I shouldn't have had to ask! If a man has a bare ring finger and asks you out on a date, he should be *single*! Now it made sense why he was so bothered by Gabe mentioning Lisa. He was pissed because he thought his friend was going to sell him out.

"I'm sorry, Toi," he said

"Why did you lie?" I asked, staring at him.

"I didn't lie," he said.

"Yes, you did!" I snapped, staring at him. "I asked you about your son's mother and you said—"

"That the story was crazy and complicated," he finished,

cutting me off.

"Well, that would have been the perfect time to say, 'Oh by the way, she's my wife!'" I yelled. "And there's nothing complicated about being married, Carlton. You either are or you aren't, there is no in between."

"You're right," he said lowly.

"So, where is your wife now?" I asked, lowering my voice.

"Home," he said.

"So while she's at home taking care of your child you're out with another woman?" I questioned sarcastically. "Wow."

"It's not like that," he said.

"Then how is it?" I asked. "Because that's how it sounds to me."

"We were having problems," he explained. "I've been staying with Robert the past couple of weeks."

"So she put you out?" I asked, with attitude. "Why? Did she catch you cheating?"

"No, I've never done this before," he said seriously. "And she didn't put me out...I left."

I listened quietly as he explained the situation leading to his and Lisa's separation. If Carlton's story was true, Lisa was a drama queen and unappreciative of what she had. However, it wasn't fair of me to judge her; I didn't know her side of the story and I hadn't walked in her shoes.

"So what's your plan?" I questioned.

"I don't know," he said, walking over and sitting on the sofa. I just know that I've been happier with you these past few days then I've been with her for the past eight months, and that's a problem."

"Whatever," I said, looking away. "If you're that miserable you would get a divorce."

"I'm telling you the truth," he said defensively. "And it's not that easy..."

"No, it's not that damn hard," I snapped, looking at him again. "If you want a divorce get a divorce. Simple."

"Toi, believe me, if I could make everything cut and dry I would," he said. "But any decision I make also affects my son. Right now he's the only reason I'm going back."

"Don't lie," I said, shaking my head. "Your son may be a factor but you love her. Don't use your child as an excuse."

"Yes, I love my wife," Carlton confessed. "But I'm not sure we can make it work. Honestly, if I thought that I could get a divorce right now without her using CJ as a ploy, I would sign right now—but that's not the case..."

"Bullshit," I laughed.

"I'm telling you the truth," he reasoned. He looked at me with eyes that seemed full of sincerity. "Right now, I don't feel like there's anything at my home for me but my son."

I don't know why I felt compelled to believe him. I mean, really? How many men had used that same line on women throughout the years? I silently asked myself those questions, but chose not to voice the concerns to him.

Carlton looked at me as if studying my facial expression, then stood and walked over to me. I watched as he knelt down before me, so that we were at eye level. "Look, I'm sorry that I didn't tell you up front," he said. "But Toi, I meant what I said...The past few days with you have been the best I've had in a long time, and I want to continue to have days like that. I want to keep getting to know you and see how far we can go. Just give me that chance. Please."

"I can't believe I'm even listening to this," I exhaled. "I should have told you to get out ten minutes ago."

"So what's stopping you?" he asked, lowly.

I couldn't answer because I didn't know why. I had no explanation as to why I had grown accustomed to a complete stranger in so little time, or why I was actually contemplating forgiving him and continuing to see him.

"I don't know," I said honestly.

Carlton leaned toward me slowly, closing the gap between us. He was close enough for our lips to brush against each other with the right movement, but far enough for our speech to be audible. My pulse began to rise, not out of anger but out of sheer sexual attraction.

"Maybe it's because you believe me," he said. "And you're not ready for this to be over."

My kitty jumped while my clit felt like it might explode from the pressure building inside of me.

"Maybe," I whispered. Or maybe it's because I wanted him at that moment and I was tired of being careful and not getting what I wanted.

He pressed his lips to mine, then slowly introduced his tongue. I spread my legs, then wrapped my arms around his neck, pulling him closer. I kissed him on the lips while pressing my breasts against his chest. As our lips shared a heated, intimate moment, he slid his hands up my thighs, underneath the dress I was wearing. His hands felt comforting to my skin as he continued to move up until he reached my panties. I broke our embrace, then leaned back in the chair while elevating my hips, allowing him to pull my undies down to my ankles, taking them off. He slowly ran his hand over my bald kitten, stroking it from one corner to the next. I spread my legs further apart, inviting him to touch the wet place in between my lips, the place that was anxiously waiting and wanting his touch.

My invitation was accepted when he began to massage the hood of my clit with his thumb. He made small, slow, circular rotations with one hand while tracing the outline of my lips with the other. I watched him, impatiently waiting for him to part my warm slit with his fingers and push inside my wet hole. I was pleasantly surprised when he lowered his head and flicked his tongue in between my pleasure fold first. At first he dipped just the tip in, like he was giving it a taste test, to see if he liked the flavor. Then he pushed the lips of my pussy open, and dove in. I moaned loudly while clutching his head in between my hands as Carlton brought me to the floodgates of satisfaction.

Just as I thought my levees might break he pulled away. He grabbed my hands then stood, pulling me up with him. I kissed him, inhaling my aroma, while stroking his hard-on through his shorts. He gasped softly when I slipped my hand in his shorts and grabbed his warm stick. As I massaged his manhood gently I could feel him growing with each pulsating second and I loved it. He grabbed my breasts through my dress, finally pulling the straps down my shoulders. He reached behind me and unhooked my bra. I slowly stripped myself of the frilly lace then tossed it to the floor. I shivered as Carlton grabbed my breasts, then licked and sucked each of my nipples before lifting my dress over my head. I helped him remove his own clothing then stood before him, admiring his body. I admired the tool between his legs. Unlike our previous encounter, this time his erection stood firm and thick.

He kissed me tenderly on the lips before lifting me up around his waist and carrying me to the sofa. He eased me down onto the sofa, while at the same time, positioning himself between my legs. I lifted my right leg, resting my ankle on top of the sofa. I wanted to grant him easy access and make sure I felt every beautiful inch of him. Carlton jolted his hips forward, attempting to slid inside of me; however, although I was slippery wet the tension in my honey pot did not allow him easy access. He looked at me and I could see in his eyes he wanted inside desperately, but he took his time slowly introducing his man to my kitten. He rocked back and forth, pushing each inch further and further past my natural barrier. Once he was content with the distance he had traveled inside of me, Carlton began to thrust and rotate his hips. I was lost inside our passion, engulfed inside our lust. He moved inside of me as if he were on a mission to find something he had been missing for far too long.

"Umm," I moaned, while wrapping my left leg around his waist. I wrapped my arms around his biceps, pressing my taunt nipples and breasts against his chest. I threw every curve he hit me with right back at him. I wanted him to know I could throw it back just as good as I could take it. Carlton held me tightly as we moved like one sweat-drenched, exotic unit. He turned his head, pressing his lips against my neck, and the feel of his warm breath on my neck caused my skin to tingle. I arched my back while groaning in ecstasy as back-to-back orgasms erupted throughout me. I could feel the waters of satisfaction in between my legs as I exhaled with delight.

I felt his muscle tighten as his rhythm increased; his beats became more intense and his breath more rugged. "Shit," he gasped, releasing his grip on me. He pulled out of my warm fountain just in time to release his warm juice on my stomach. "Damn…" he groaned, kissing me roughly on the lips. "Damn…"

In that moment of euphoria, I realized I had no idea what I was doing or where I thought my relationship with Carlton could possibly go. The only thing I was certain of was that it was completely outside of everything I had ever practiced, I liked it, and I wanted more.

# Chapter 13

## Lisa

It was on days like today that I was thankful I had a job to go to. Otherwise I would have been sitting at home, miserable and in a slump thinking about my husband and our problems. I've heard 1,001 times that you don't miss your water until your well runs dry, and I was living proof that the saying was true. I didn't know if Carlton was trying to teach me a lesson or if his heart was no longer with me but either way, I was missing having him home terribly.

I stayed at the shop until my aunt closed, and I finally had no choice but to go home. To give me a break she offered to let CJ spend the night with her. I wanted to decline out of selfishness because I didn't want to be alone, but CJ begged to go. It was just after eight when I made it home, and the only thing I wanted to do was take a hot shower, then climb into bed. I pulled up in my driveway and immediately felt my heart skip a beat. Carlton's car sat in the driveway, parked in his normal spot.

I smoothed my hands down over my hair, attempting to pat each strand in place. I took my time getting out of my car and walking up the walkway leading to the door. I opened the front door and found Carlton stretched out on the sofa. He wore a pair of grey basketball shorts and a white tank top. In one hand he held a Corona bottle; in the other, the TV remote. He looked at me carefully, as if he was examining me with his eyes before sitting up straight.

"Hey," he said, sitting his drink and the remote down on the coffee table in front of him.

"Hi." I stepped inside the living room, slowly closing the door behind me.

"Where's CJ?"

"He went home with Ellen," I said. "If I had known you were going to be here, I would have brought him home."

"It's cool," he said. "I tried to call you but I got your voicemail."

"I didn't get it," I said, digging in my purse until I retrieved my cell phone. I suddenly felt the need to justify everything. "My battery…it's dead," I said, holding up my phone as proof. "I meant to put it on the charger but I forgot. I just left the shop." I was rambling out of sheer nervousness. I walked over to the kitchen, pulled out the top drawer where I kept my cell phone charger, then plugged it in the wall outlet. I could feel Carlton watching my every move. I turned slowly, then redirected my attention to him as I stepped back into the living room.

"Sorry," I said again.

"It's cool," he said. "It gave me some extra time to get my thoughts together. Listen," he started, clasping his hands together. "I can't continue to do this."

*He's going to ask me for a divorce*, I immediately thought.

"I always told you that I didn't want our son to have the kind of childhood I had. Yelling. Screaming. Police knocking on our door." He looked at me with raised eyebrows.

Carlton's parents were still together, but I had forgotten tales he once shared with me of his troubled childhood. According to Carlton, his mother Gladys and his father Earl would fight over any and everything. From who drank all the orange juice to who was hogging the TV remote. Carlton said what should have been minor disagreements would escalate into knock-down drag-outs, until someone was bleeding or the neighbors called the cops.

"Carlton, I'm so sorry about that," I said, desperately. "I was mad and I was angry and…and in my mind…I was telling myself that I was right. I know…I get a little crazy and…and I do things, bad things but—"

"Let me finish," he said, cutting me off.

I bit down on my bottom lip while nodding in agreement.

"I'm not going to allow CJ to grow up in an environment where he feels like he has to play referee between the two of us. And I damn sure ain't going to let him see me putting my hands on his mother or any other woman, for that fact. Nor will I allow him to see his father be disrespected again. Do you understand?" The look in his eyes provided me unspoken confirmation that the next time I chose to hit, punch, and possibly even kick Carlton he could possibly retaliate.

"I was wrong for hitting you," I confessed. "But you made me so—"

"I don't care what you think I did or didn't do," he said firmly. "The next time you decide to raise your hand at me, I promise you, you'll have a reason to dial 911." There was an undercurrent to his tone that had me slightly shaken. For the first time since we had gotten together, he inflicted fear in me.

"Okay," I said, slowly. "I understand."

"I'll be honest," he said, in a gentler tone than what he had used just seconds earlier. "If it wasn't for CJ I wouldn't be here. He's the only reason I came back."

"And that's fine," I said, abruptly. "If he's the only reason, then right now that's reason enough." At that moment I didn't care why he was home, I was just glad to have him. At least now I had the chance to prove myself. That's all I wanted and all I needed.

"Now that you're back, we can get it all back," I said convincingly. I made the short distance from the door to the sofa, then sat down beside my husband. I exhaled, relieved that he was home and yes, that he had given us another chance.

"We can start all over again," I continued.

He frowned slightly before looking away.

"You don't have to say anything," I reassured him. "Just wait; I'll prove it." There was an uncomfortable silence looming between us until I finally said, "I'm going to go hop in the shower. I'll be right back." I stood while staring at him. "I'm glad you're home."

He nodded his head in agreement.

Three minutes later I stood in our shower, allowing the steady flow of warm water to saturate me from head to toe. I watched as the suds from the body wash I had used for lather swirled down the drain. I tilted my head back and closed my eyes while smiling victoriously. My husband was home. Finally! After standing under the water until it turned cold, I climbed out, then wrapped a large towel around me. I made my way back to the living room still soaking wet. I decided there was no better way to welcome my man back than with a little reminder of what he had at home: some good loving. Carlton sat on the sofa staring at the television as I entered wearing nothing but a towel and a smile.

"I'm ready."

He looked from the TV to me. "Ready for what?" he inquired.

"Whatever you like," I said, lowering my eyes. I opened the towel slowly, then allowed it to fall to the floor. I stood with a hand on my hip. "However you like."

"You know, I'm going to need a rain check," he said, unfazed by my body. "I'm a little tired. It's been a long day." He looked me directly in my eyes, not once glancing at my naked body. I found his reaction odd but I decided not to make too much of it. We still had some barriers to work through and I knew I had to be patient.

"No problem," I said, picking up the towel. "I understand. Maybe later?" I secured the towel back around my breasts, then smiled.

"Yeah," he said, looking back at the TV.

"Okay." I turned to walk away, then paused. "I love you," I said.

He looked at me and smiled. "I love you too," he said.

Despite my embarrassment from being turned down while I was butt-ass naked and soaking wet, I took refuge in his words and I could feel the sincerity in them.

*****

I woke up in the middle of the night and discovered I was in bed alone. I stretched, then dragged myself out of bed. As I approached the living room, I could hear the TV and what I thought was Carlton's muffled voice. Once I made it to the living room, I saw the TV was on, but Carlton lay stretched out on the sofa sound asleep. I turned the television off but chose not to disturb my husband.

As I turned to leave the room, I heard what sounded like a number being pressed. I turned around then looked at Carlton again. He didn't move an inch. I looked around a few minutes for his cell phone, but it was nowhere in sight. I headed back up the hall to our bedroom, leaving the door open once I was inside.

As I climbed back into bed I looked at the nightstand on Carlton's side of the bed. The holster he carried his phone in lay in the open with his phone secured in it. I brushed it off, thinking I was hearing things. After all, who would Carlton have to talk to at this time in the morning? What time is it? I thought. I lifted my head to look at the alarm clock on my nightstand and saw that it was 3:30 am. I also saw the small indicator light on the cordless phone base beside it go from red to green: an indication that the line had been in use and was now free.

# Chapter 14

## Toi

The bond that Carlton and I had developed was one I felt could survive even if we never slept together again and decided only to be friends. He was someone I felt I could talk to about anything, and he told me he felt the same about me. Although A-Ex had assigned him a new route, Carlton made sure we got to see each other almost every day. Sometimes it was a quick visit on his lunch break; mostly it was after work. On the weekends I counted it as a guarantee that one night, if only a few hours, was dedicated to me. If there was a free moment to be made, he made it and I enjoyed every second of it. I got more time than I would expect a woman in my position to receive, but it was never too much. I had concluded that he was torn about leaving Lisa. I knew and he admitted he loved her, but there was something missing. I think I had that something but Lisa had one thing I didn't: she had his child.

The corporate office of Fashionista decided we would be open only half of the day on Memorial Day. Since I had no plans and it was already such a short day, I decided to give my employees the day off and man the store alone. As it was already 2:30 pm and I had only one customer, I felt I'd made the right choice. I was in the middle of straightening the ladies' dresses for what had to be my fifth time that day, when Carlton stopped by, dressed in shorts and a Nike T-shirt. He held a carry-out plate in his hands and was smiling, showing off his dimples.

"And to what do I owe the pleasure of this visit?" I questioned, greeting him.

"I wanted to see you," he said, giving me a peck on the lips. "And I brought you lunch."

"That was sweet of you," I gushed appreciatively. I took the Styrofoam container from his hands and opened the lid. Inside there were grilled chicken wings, shrimp, and a baked potato loaded with cheese and bacon bits. It looked good and smelled delicious.

"You cooked this?" I asked, walking to the sales counter. I picked up a shrimp and bit into it. I was breaking my "no eating on the floor" policy, but that was one of the perks of being the boss; I could bend a rule or two when necessary.

"Yes," he said proudly.

"This is delicious," I said honestly. I covered my mouth as I chewed.

"So where is everyone?" he asked, looking around the store.

"I'm working alone today," I confessed, while closing the lid on the plate. I sat the container on the counter by the register. "And business is so slow it's ridiculous." I continued. "I haven't had a customer in over two hours."

Carlton looked at me with a gleam in his eyes and his eyebrows raised. "So, I could do whatever I wanted to you right now and no one would be the wiser?" he asked suggestively.

"No...no you can't," I said firmly. "Not here."

A look of disappointment fell over his face.

"The break room," I said mischievously "No cameras."

"Are you serious?" he asked, showing his dimples.

I answered his question when I went and locked the front doors. "Are you coming?" I asked, leading the way.

"Hell, yes," he replied, quickly following me.

As soon as we reached the room I was all over him, kissing and groping him passionately. The sound of his cell phone ringing interrupted our make-out session, but only temporarily. I waited patiently for Carlton to answer; he didn't. Instead he removed the device from his pocket, silencing the tone and tossing it on a nearby table.

I quickly unbuttoned his shorts, then pulled them along with his boxers down around his ankles. I waited for him to step out of them both before gently dropping them to the floor.

"Sit down," I commanded.

He pulled out a plastic folding chair from under the table and sat down as instructed. I kissed him hard on the mouth, giving just a taste of my tongue before easing down on my knees. He was semi-hard but I planned to get him to full staff in sixty seconds or less. I grabbed his chocolate wood and greeted it with my open lips and wet tongue. I sucked fast and hard, wetting Carlton's dick from the base to the head.

"Damn," he moaned, flinching.

I felt his muscles tighten as I shook my head back and forth wildly while rolling my tongue back and forth against his stick. I sucked my jaws in around his stiffness, slowly easing my way up to his head, then plunging down to the base. I stayed there for a brief moment, then pulled away and looked up at Carlton. He looked down at me with his mouth open. I smiled, assuming he was impressed and because my mission had been accomplished.

I pulled the pencil skirt I wore up around my waist and quickly removed my panties. I straddled his lap before easing down onto his erection. I rocked and rolled my hips, grinding against Carlton as if my life depended on it. I sucked his earlobe while moaning softly in his ear as he held on to my waist and matched me stroke for stroke. I rode Carlton's dick like I was on a stallion in the midst of a high-speed chase.

"You feel good," he moaned.

"You feel better," I said, honestly.

"Turn around," he ordered.

I strategically rotated on his stick until my back was facing him. I pulled my legs together in between his, then planted my feet on the floor and one hand on each of his kneecaps. My new position left me vulnerable to every inch Carlton had to give and he fed each and every one of those inches to me properly.

"Fuck," he blurted. "Shiiiit…"

"Mmm," I moaned, leaning back against his chest. I looked back into his eyes before kissing him slowly. He pulled away, then placed his hand on my back and pushed me forward so that my head was in between my legs. I grabbed my ankles while biting my bottom lip. Carlton pounded me so hard it felt like he was pushing 200+ pounds of his weight inside me via his stick.

"Yesss!" I screamed, reaching my peak.

"Here it comes, baby…" Carlton groaned. "Here it comes…"

He increased the speed of his thrust. "Toi," he moaned. The sound of him calling my name was like music to my ears.

# CHAPTER 15

## Lisa

When I questioned Carlton about the phone the night he returned home, he advised me that he had fallen asleep while attempting to reset his voice mail. He said that he woke up and realized the phone was in between the sofa cushions, hung up, then fell back asleep. I believed him but I wanted to be 100% sure there was no reason for me to doubt him, so after he left for work the next morning, I hit redial on the phone. When Carlton answered, I had my confirmation. I played off the call by telling him I had forgotten to say I love you and that was the end of the subject.

Since then, there hadn't been any other situations or incidences that sent up my radar. I was happy and I felt we were finally on the right road again. I advised Carlton he could invite his friends over to help celebrate the Memorial Day holiday but he chose not to. I was pleased as well as relieved. Granted, I would have played the happy hostess but the truth was, his friends much like his family, somewhat annoyed me. The only thing I had in common with either of the parties was Carlton and CJ, and in my opinion, that was not enough to pretend. Don't get me wrong, in the beginning of our relationship I would have broken my back to be accepted by his family and his friends and in a way I did. I went to every barbecue, birthday party, and game night his friend Quinton and his girl Nesha had, and I had even forged a friendship with Nesha. However, once I settled into my divine spot, I felt no need to continue our bond.

Besides, I didn't like the fact that Nesha was so close to Carlton. The two of them spent entirely too much time together. When she had problems, she called Carlton. When she had car trouble, she called Carlton. When I asked if anything ever transpired between them, Carlton said no, but I still didn't dig the connection. People claimed men and women could have purely platonic bonds, but in my opinion, that's a load of crap. If a straight man is friends with a straight woman they are either screwing or one of them wants to. I felt the only males and females capable of maintaining a platonic friendship are children, and hell, even that's before they hit puberty. Therefore, in my opinion, Nesha and Carlton's little bond had to be broken.

Carlton's friend Gabe was another story: I liked him and the way he carried himself. I wasn't fond of his choice of lifestyle (the man made all his money illegally), but he was more mature and I trusted that if he and Carlton went out he wouldn't be throwing slut after slut in my husband's face, unlike his cousin Robert.

I looked at my watch, wondering what was taking Carlton so long. After he finished grilling, he showered, then said he was going to take his aunt some of the food he cooked.

"Is Martha going to be able to eat all that?" I questioned, staring at the two plates he had prepared.

"If not, she'll have some for tomorrow," he said. "I'll be back."

He kissed CJ on his forehead then departed. That was two

hours ago. I decided to wait a few more minutes before giving him a courtesy call. I sat out on the patio with the latest edition of *Cosmopolitan* magazine flipped open on my lap. I was more interested in watching CJ run back and forth through the sprinklers than I was with columns and articles. I was so tired of the same sugary sweet advice columns on how to please a man. A man's satisfaction boils down to two things: screw him and screw him some more. Since Carlton and I made up and I've been more willing to give him sex whenever he desires, things have been great. In fact, now that I was offering it more he seemed to be content with less. So my conclusion was, if you want your man to be satisfied, give him some or at least be willing. There is no secret formula.

I laughed while observing that CJ was in a world of his own as he jumped and hopped back and forth through the water barefoot, wearing nothing put a pair of SpongeBob SquarePants swim trunks. The cordless sitting on the small bistro table next to me began to ring. I picked up the handset, checking the caller ID before answering. Martha's name and phone number came up on-screen, I assumed it was Carlton calling to check in.

"Lisa, it's Martha," Martha said from the other end of the phone.

"Hey, Martha," I said. I couldn't resist the urge to roll my eyes. Martha's voice just had that effect on me.

"Listen, I just wanted to thank you for the food," she said. "It was so good. I ate and wanted to call you before sleep crept up on me." She laughed. "I told Carlton that next time I'll have to come over and bring a dish."

"Sounds good," I lied.

"Well, I'll let you go—"

"Martha, can I speak to Carlton?" I asked politely. I wanted to know when he planned to return home.

"He's not here, baby," she said.

"How long ago did he leave?" I asked, curious.

"'Bout an hour."

"Thanks for calling, Martha," I said. "Talk to you later."

"Bye-bye," she said.

I ended the call, then immediately dialed Carlton's cell phone. The line rang three times before he answered. I waited for him to say hello but he never did. Instead there was interference and noise. It sounded like he was fumbling with the phone or moving.

Did he drop the phone? I thought while shaking my head.

"Hello," I said. "Hellooo, Carlton…"

The interference stopped and I heard distorted noises in the background before finally hearing a woman's voice.

"Sit down," she said.

I could hear the sound of something screeching, what sounded like a chair moving across a floor. A few seconds later I heard what sounded like lips smacking and a man moaning. When I heard a man say, "Damn," I instantly recognized the voice of my husband. As I continued to listen I felt my pulse began to race. The noises and sounds I was hearing were clear. The sounds of smacking, slapping, and gushing echoed in my ear and began to speak to my brain. I felt like I was going to lose my lunch, as I continued to listen helplessly.

"You feel so good," he moaned.

"You feel better," she said.

I clutched my stomach as tears formed in my eyes. I felt a knot of pain and agony in my gut. This wasn't right. Certainly I was hearing things wrong. He wouldn't. He couldn't. He would never cheat on me!

"Turn around," Carlton said gruffly.

Visualizing my husband with his dick in another woman caused my head to ache and my heart to beat erratically. I began pacing back and forth across the patio. Their pounding and deep breathing played over the phone like horrible music flowing through stereo speakers.

"Fuck," he yelled out. "Shit!"

"Mmm," she moaned.

"Yesss!" she screamed, engulfed in their passion.

I felt myself hyperventilating as I clutched the phone in my hand.

"Here it comes, baby…" he groaned. "Here it comes…."

The sound of Carlton cumming made my knees weak. I had never heard him sound so passionate, never so pleased. I cried silently almost choking on my tears. I thought that the moment could not get worse that I heard the worst thing anyone could ever hear until he did something for her he had never done for me. He called out her name in ecstasy.

"Toi," he moaned.

I listened to Carlton and his slut until they finished. "I'll call you tonight," he promised her.

"You really shouldn't take these kinds of chances," she said. She sounded so innocent, so concerned. If she was *that* innocent or concerned, she wouldn't be screwing my husband! I had never heard her voice or her name before, but I knew I would never be able to forget either of them.

"I'll find a way," he vowed.

"Okay," she said, cheerfully. I could tell the whore was smiling, undoubtedly pleased. "Thank you again for the food," she said. "That was so thoughtful." That dirty muthafucker! I thought.

"Anytime, baby," Carlton replied. "Thank you for…you know."

She laughed. "I take it you're pleased?" she asked.

"You know I am," he said. I could feel his ass smiling through the phone.

"You're most welcome," she said. I could hear footsteps as their voices moved further away.

"Baby, don't forget your phone," she said. The sound of heels tapping across the floor came closer and then the line went dead.

*****

My eyes burned from the mascara-coated tears I had shed during and even after the phone call. I had never felt so betrayed. So hurt. How long had he been cheating one me? I thought. Who was she? I questioned. What did she look like?

I sat in our living room asking myself those questions over and over again. The questions were torture within themselves, almost more so than hearing Carlton banging another chick. I felt sick to my stomach as the sounds replayed in my head. Maybe it wasn't what I thought. Maybe it was something else, something less horrible. I wanted to convince myself that I had jumped to conclusions, misinterpreted the obvious. I wanted to but I couldn't, just like I couldn't hide my pain when he walked through the door.

"What's wrong?" he asked immediately, as he stepped across the threshold.

I was almost unable to bear the sight of him. I sat silently, shaking my head as my tears began to flow again. I swiped them away with the back of my hands.

"Where's CJ?" he asked, looking around. "Did something happen to him?" I remained silent while he stared at me. "Lisa," he demanded. "Where is my son?" He headed in the direction of CJ's bedroom. I listened as he opened the bedroom door, then finally closed it.

A few seconds later he returned, staring at me in the living room. There was relief in his eyes, I'm sure from discovering that our son was in his bedroom sleeping peacefully.

"Lisa, what's wrong with you?" He asked, observing me closely.

"I called you," I said. "To see what was taking you so long."

"Is that what this is about?" he asked gently. "Why you're so upset?" I nodded my head yes.

"I was busy helping Aunt Martha move her TV," he sighed, shaking his head. He walked over to the kitchen, then dropped his keys on the table. "I heard the phone ring but I couldn't get to it." He opened the refrigerator, removing a bottle of water. I watched as he twisted open the cap and took several long sips.

*Fucking around on your wife must make you thirsty*, I thought.

"The time flew by before I knew it," he said. He pulled out one of the wooden chairs and sat down at the table. "Is that all?" he asked.

"No," I said, through clenched teeth. "That's not all."

"What else? I didn't return your call so you're pissed?" he asked. "I thought we were past your tantrums about me spending time with my family." He sounded so arrogant, so cocky. He was completely oblivious to what he had done and how he had hurt me.

"Don't play with me, Carlton," I snapped. "I heard you! Over the phone with that bitch!"

He sat up straight in his hair, looking at me. "What are you talking about?"

"When I called, you accidentally picked up," I informed him. "I heard *everything*." I breathed deeply while glaring at him. He continued to stare at me as if he didn't have a clue what I was talking about.

"Heard what?"

"You were with her," I said. "With Toi…" At the mere mention of her name, I saw something in his eyes. "The two of you were having sex," I said. "I heard you…moaning and screwing her. I heard you when you said her name!" He continued to stare at me but offered no explanation or apologies.

"You're not going to even try and deny it?" I asked.

"No," he said, blankly.

"Who is she?" I questioned, through my tears.

"A friend——"

"That you're screwing," I said, sarcastically. "How long, Carlton?"

"About a month."

"Is she…the first?"

"Yes," he answered.

"I can't believe this," I said, standing. "Do you know how bad you've hurt me?"

"I'm sorry," he said, calmly.

"That's it?" I asked, shaking my head. "You're sorry?"

"Yes," he said. He was calm and collected, like he was unfazed by the seriousness of what he had done. It was almost like he was trying to get back at me. Trying to get even. As I stared at him I thought of the mistakes I had made. Was this Karma coming back to haunt me?

"Where did you meet her? When?" I asked, lowly.

"It doesn't matter where we met and she's not interested in being friends."

"Yes, it does matter!" I snapped. "It matters to me!"

"Knowing won't change anything," he said raising his voice.

"Nothing."

He was right, it wasn't going to change anything. But I still wanted to know.

"Were you trying to hurt me?" I questioned through my tears. "Is that why you did it?"

"No," he said, exhaling. "I didn't do it to hurt you. I did it for me."

"Why?"

"I met her and she was different."

The way he spoke of Toi bothered me. Not once did he say that it was just sex, that he was just screwing her. I looked at him, wondering if it was possible that my husband had developed feelings for the woman.

"Are you in love with her, Carlton?" I asked, nervously.

He looked at me, hesitated and then shook his head. "No," he said.

What he didn't say was that he had feelings for her, but I saw that in his face. Maybe it was nothing more than a crush or maybe she was just a good piece of ass. Either way there was more behind his eyes than I was able to read.

"I suggest you end it, if you want to continue sharing a home with your son," I ordered, wiping my eyes. "And you better end it now, because I won't hesitant to pack our shit and leave your ass." I looked at him and hoped he was taking me seriously. "Do you understand?" I asked.

He looked at me, then nodded his head. I knew threatening to take CJ was the one thing that would make Carlton come back to his senses and quickly. I marched out of the room to our bedroom then slammed the door behind me. I stood with my back against the bedroom door and my hands covering my face. I used CJ as an ultimatum because the truth was, after seeing the look in Carlton's eyes when he talked about Toi, I wasn't a 100% sure that he would have chosen me over her.

*****

I waited until I heard Carlton go into the guest bathroom and run water from the faucet before coming out of our bedroom. I went straight to his phone on the coffee table. I touched the screen, then scrolled the contacts until I found the letter that interested me: the letter T.

"Hello," she answered cheerfully after I dialed.

"Toi?" I asked. I was 50% sure it was her but I wanted to 100%.

She paused, shocked to hear my voice instead of Carlton's, I'm sure. "Yes," she said. She sounded completely professional. I guess much like looks, voices can be deceiving too.

"This is Lisa," I said. I channeled all of my inner strength in an attempt to remain calm. "Carlton's *wife*." I put emphasis on the word *wife* to remind her of whom she was: the whore.

"Hello, Lisa," she said calmly. "What can I do for you?"

"You can stay away from my husband," I replied. "Can you do that for me, please?" I originally planned to build up to my request but considering she asked, I figured there was no need to beat around the bush.

"Lisa, whatever goes on between you and Carlton is between the two of you," she said.

"That's not what I asked you, I asked you to stay away from my husband," I reminded her. "Now, I'm asking you again… politely… Stay away from my husband."

"Have a good night, Lisa," she said, before hanging up.

No she didn't just dismiss me! Really? I pressed the call button on his phone twice, calling her again.

"Yes?"

"Listen, you little home-wrecking bitch—" I whispered.

"Just for today I'll be that bitch," she said loudly. "Just because I know you're going through something...However, a home wrecker I am not. Your marriage was falling apart way before I stepped into the picture. And we both know you can't wreck something that's already broke down and waiting for a jump-off."

"Go to hell," I said. I pressed end call on his phone and slammed it on the table. I marched back to my bedroom as her words echoed in my head. Maybe the problem was my husband, but I had come to her as a woman and it was in her best interest to honor my request.

G STREET CHRONICLES
A NEW URBAN DYNASTY
WWW.GSTREETCHRONICLES.COM

# Chapter 16

## Toi

I hadn't considered what would happen in the event that Lisa found out about our affair; hell, I hadn't had time. The two of us had just started dating. Wasn't it a little early for shit to be hitting the fan? However, from her phone call and the grim look on Carlton's face when he came by to visit me the next morning, it was obvious that it had.

"She knows about us," he said, stepping through the doorway.

"I know," I said calmly. "She called me."

"When?"

"Last night," I advised him. "From your phone."

"What did she say?"

"The basics, keep away from her husband," I said. "How did she find out?" I questioned.

"Yesterday, when we were in the break room she called," he explained. "I thought I was sending her to voice mail but I accidentally answered instead."

"She heard us talking?" I concluded.

He shook his head, "Worst," he said. "She heard us while we were—"

"Oh," I said, cutting him off. "Wow...So what happened

when you got home?" I listened quietly as Carlton gave me a breakdown of his conversation with Lisa and the ultimatum she gave him. Once he finished he looked at me with a solemn expression on his face. I came to my own conclusion of what his look meant.

"So you came to tell me it's over," I said. I kept my tone light and pleasant. I was disappointed, but I didn't want to make him any more uncomfortable than I imagined he already was. I wanted him to know that I would get over my disappointment and we would still be cool. I knew he had to do what he had to for his son. I may have been disrespecting his marriage and helping him disrespect his vows, but there was something to be said about a father's love.

"What?" He frowned. "No. Why? Do you want it to be over?"

"No, I just assumed..."

"You assumed wrong," he said soothingly. "You can't get rid of me that fast. I just wanted to let you know that the calls and time may be a little short until things cool down."

"Oh," I said, smiling. "That's not an issue...I mean, I understand." Certainly the man

couldn't get right back to his old ways so soon. I understood that.

He smiled for the first time, then stepped closer. "Thank you for understanding," he said, stroking my cheek with his fingertips. "I'll call you on my lunch break."

"Okay," I said, giving him a quick hug.

"Bye baby," he said, before walking out the door.

*****

By noon it was as if someone had opened the shoppers' floodgates. The store was packed and we were getting slammed with back-to-back transactions. I wasn't complaining; the more money the store made, the bigger my bonus. My employees were handling the rush like troopers and I couldn't be more proud of them. Chloe keyed the sales transactions, while Kathy, one of my part-time associates, bagged customers' merchandise. I walked along the sales floor assisting customers, answering questions, and looking out for potential shoplifters. The crowd of shoppers slowly began to thin out enough that I could focus on straightening the disheveled racks and tables of clothes without any distractions. I was lost in my own thoughts refolding a table of ladies' baby tees when I looked up and saw Gabe walking toward me wearing a silk short-sleeved shirt, Ray-Bans, and poplin pants. What does he want? I asked myself.

"Ms. Toi," he said, stopping beside me.

"How's it going, Gabe?"

Gabe was the last person I expected to see. Carlton advised me that Gabe apologized for the name dropping at the barbeque, and stated that he thought Carlton had already told me about Lisa at the time. Carlton said the two of them came to a mutual agreement to put the situation behind him, but I still felt Gabe had violated some form of man law. There were some things you just didn't do, and call your boy out was one of them. I felt it wasn't my place to voice my opinion on their friendship or what I felt was a lack thereof, so I kept my thoughts to myself about the situation but in my opinion Gabe was a bitch.

"Everything is everything, it's a blessing to be in the presence of your royalty and shined upon with your beauty," he said, smiling. "Life is love and love is good."

"Oh, okay," I said, folding the last shirt. I wondered if he was high or if his ultimate goal was to come off as a philosophical pimp. If his choice was the latter, I would definitely have to say his mission was accomplished. "So what can I do for you?"

"Can you step outside for a minute?" He asked. "Kindly give me a minute of your air."

I didn't want to be bothered with Gabe, not to mention I had tons of other things I needed to do. However, I didn't want to be rude.

"It'll only take a minute," he said, removing his shades. "Please…"

His eyes were lowered and slightly glassy which answered my first question, Yes, he was high. I looked at my watch and decided it was time for a break.

"Sure," I said politely. "Give me a second."

After advising my employees that I was going on break, I joined Gabe outside in the parking lot.

"So, what's up?" I questioned, looking at him.

"I want to apologize for my behavior when you came to my place of residence," he explained. "It was never my intent to be rude."

"Apology accepted."

"I hope that this will in no way hinder what I hope the two of us can build," he continued, while staring at me.

"And that is?"

"A beautiful friendship," he answered. "And anything else we deem appropriate." He raised his eyebrows slightly while putting emphasis on the word *else*.

"I've already told you that I won't allow you to do business in front of my store," I said, assuming that he was referring to his desire to sell his merchandise in the parking lot.

"Oh, no worries," he said quickly. "I've chosen another location not far from here. I'm good where that's concerned. However, I figure there may be other areas that the two of us may want to explore..."

He smiled mischievously. What the hell? It was obvious that he was making a play and hitting on me.

"I think that we are better off leaving things as they are," I said, politely. "You're Carlton's friend—"

"And what exactly are you?" he asked, cutting me off.

*I'm none of your damn business*, I thought to myself.

"You should ask him," I responded.

"I see," he said, nodding his head. "So this means that you are available and open to the possibilities of new friendships. Free to give other deserving and less attached gentlemen a chance."

I was almost at a loss for words. Gabe *was* hitting on me and he was doing so without shame. I would have been completely at a loss until I reminded myself to whom I was talking. This was the same so-called friend that inquired about his homeboy's wife in front of his date.

"I'm free to give other men a chance," I said firmly. "However, I prefer those men not to be friends with the man I'm currently... friends with...I don't get down like that."

"But you do get down with the married brothers?" he asked sarcastically. "Somewhat of a twisted ethical policy you practice."

It was obvious that I had offended him by turning him down. It was also obvious that he was a hater and was attempting to push my buttons.

"This from the man who sells stolen merchandise for a living," I said, raising my eyebrows. He looked at me then frowned. I watched as he put his sunglasses back on. He slowly licked his bottom lip, then smiled.

"You can't blame a brother for trying," he said. "Nor can I blame a sistah for declining." He extended his hand to me. I reached out to shake his hand.

"No, you can't," I said, giving his hand a shake.

He held my hand in his longer than what I considered to be appropriate, then finally turned my hand over, raised it to his lips, and kissed it. I pulled away quickly, then looked at my watch.

"I better get back to work," I said. "Thanks for stopping by."

"I guess the disappointment as well as the pleasure is all mine," he laughed lightly. "I'll see you around."

By the close of business I was exhausted but happy with our sales for the day. I pulled in front of my building with two things on my mind: a long hot bath and sleep. I loved living at Emerald Ridge for many reasons, but the security and beauty of the complex were my top two. I strolled down the sidewalk toward my door while admiring how the rows of brightly lit, miniature streetlights reflected off the leaves of the neatly trimmed hedges. I entered the breezeway and found a long, metallic gift box laying across my welcome mat.

"Aww," I said, bending down to pick up the box.

Thoughts of Carlton immediately entered my mind as I slipped the small paper card from underneath the shiny red ribbon that loosely secured the box. The lid of the box was slightly ajar and I could see the blooms of the red roses inside. The message inside the card simply read: *Thinking of you. XOXO Carlton.*

"So sweet," I gushed, balancing the box and my bag in one hand and unlocking the door with the other. I immediately dropped everything on my coffee table before plopping down on the sofa. Rubbing my feet slowly I stared at the box. I loved surprises and Carlton's was right on time. The only other thing that could have made my night better was if he were there with me. I pushed the lid of the box open, then screamed while climbing backward onto the back of the sofa. A small green snake slithered across the buds of the roses and finally over the box's edge onto my coffee table.

*****

The on duty courtesy officer, James, was kind enough to come to my rescue and capture the snake. This was only after I called him screaming as if I were being tortured. I didn't give a damn that the snake was nonpoisonous and barely as long as my forearm. It was a snake and I hated reptiles in all forms.

"He probably slid in the box because it was cool," James explained.

I made a mental note to advise Carlton to never ever leave anything on my doorstep again and if he did to at least make sure the box is closed! Then I would properly thank him for being such a sweetheart. I took a nice hot bath to calm my muscles and my nerves. I stood in my bathroom mirror massaging shea butter all over my skin when I got this unsettling feeling. I shook it off as nerves and the fact that I was still reeling from the discovery of my unwanted pet inside my bouquet. As I stalked from my bathroom into my bedroom, enjoying my naked freedom, the feeling grew with every second. I pulled my favorite Alabama T-shirt out of my dresser then slipped it over my head before turning off the light and climbing into bed.

My bottom had barely made contact with the sheets when I heard a crash coming from my living room. I eased out of bed, grabbing my cell phone off the nightstand in the process.

I paused by the bedroom door listening for movement. When I didn't hear any, I tiptoed down the hall. My heart raced erratically as I leaned up against the wall waiting. After a few seconds that felt like eternity, I stepped out into the open, then flipped the light on.

I was relieved to find that I was alone; however, there was a bright red brick lying next to my sofa, and the glass that once housed the bay window in my living room now lay broken and scattered across the carpeted floor.

*****

"Do you think she did it?" LaShay asked. "Followed him to your spot when he dropped off the flowers and lost it?"

"Who else would have?" I asked, shaking my head.

The two of us sat in her living room curled up on each corner of her couch, discussing my drama, from Lisa overhearing Carlton and I together to her phone call to the harassment at my home that night. After I'd discovered the broken window I dialed James and he called in for an on-duty officer. Together they inspected the scene in and around my unit. When asked if I knew of anyone who would want to damage my property, I advised them no. When James asked me to step outside so that he could show me something, I dropped Lisa's name like a hotcake.

"We got some fresh footprints," James said. He held a flashlight so that the low beam illuminated the ground underneath and leading to my window seal. "Right here you can see the shoe imprint. Whoever was standing here was a woman."

I nodded my head in agreement while staring at the imprints in the ground that matched perfectly to the bottom of high heels.

James boarded up my window for the night, but I still chose to sleep elsewhere.

"That's a bad chick," LaShay said, shaking her head. "Snakes. Busting out windows and shit in heels. Now me personally, I would have worn my sneaks so I had some grips to run. I mean y—"

"Shay!" I cut her off. "

"My bad," she said. "So what are you going to do?"

"I don't know," I said, honestly. "I can't prove it was her. Hell, I can't even prove she knows where I live. Without a witness or a confession that she did it…"

"You're screwed," LaShay finished for me.

"Basically," I said, defeated. "I don't know what to do. All I know is, I don't need this type of drama. I'm not built for the bullshit."

# Chapter 17

## Lisa

Days later my mind was still consumed with thoughts of my husband and the things I had heard taking place between him and Toi. So much so, that I chose not to go to the salon and took the rest of the week off. I pulled myself out of bed just long enough to kiss CJ good-bye before he left with his father then crawled back underneath the covers. I planned to do absolutely nothing until it was time for me to pick up CJ from day care.

I lay in bed with my eyes closed, trying my best to go back to sleep, but after a couple of hours of restlessness I finally decided to get up and do a little Web surfing. I took a long, hot shower, washed my hair, then slipped on a pair of grey shorts and a grey tank top and my flip-flops. I dragged my feet as I walked across the house to the spare bedroom, where we kept our computer. Carlton had slept in the spare room after I locked him out of our room and refused to open the door. After that, I went into total lockdown which meant no cooking, washing his drawers, or anything in between. I refused to even talk to Carlton. I understood that he and I were now even—he cheated and so had I—but it didn't make me feel any less like shit about his affair.

I eased down in the small office chair, then logged on to the PC. After checking out the latest news on the Google homepage I decided to check in on Facebook. I wasn't big on the whole social media revolution, but I did have a page that I checked every few months just to see what the people I knew were up to. It amazed me how a simple status update or post on the site was capable of ruining a person's entire life. People aired their business like dirty laundry on a line. I noticed that my sister Monica was also online and she had posted a few new pictures of my nephews. I dropped a positive comment about the pictures before logging off.

I decided to check our family e-mail account before shutting down the computer and I'm glad I did; the mailbox was filled with nothing but spam. I cleared the in-box, then decided to set up spam filters. I was almost done with my mission when I heard a tiny ding and was greeted by a pop-up box. The message inside the little grey box read, "Good morning" and I saw that the sender of the instant message was a user by the name of ToiUwood1000.

At the sight of her name, I knew who it was and I wanted to drive my fist through the glass of the monitor…but I managed to maintain my composure. "He got his broad instant messaging and shit," I grumbled while debating whether or not to respond.

Why was she still hitting Carlton up? I know he told her they couldn't see each other again, right? Maybe she was only chatting. If so, she needed to find someone else to talk to. I decided to respond to see exactly what she wanted.

*Me: Good morning.*

ToiUwood1000: I'm all smiles right now!

Who gives a damn, I thought.

*Me: Are you?*

*ToiUwood1000: Yes, I am. I miss you, Daddy.*

Daddy?

*Me: Do you really?*

*ToiUwood1000: Yes, I can't wait to show you how much.*

The thought of how she planned to *show* Carlton made my stomach turn. I stared at the screen with thoughts running through my head of Toi and Carlton. My thoughts became almost unbearable.

*ToiUwood100: Hello...Babe, are you still there?*

*Me: I just have one question*

*ToiUwood1000: ?*

*Me: How do you sleep at night?*

*ToiUwood1000: Good, after I've been with you. (Smiles)*

*Me: Is that right?*

*ToiUwood1000: You know it is*

*Me: Tell me something?*

*ToiUwood1000: Anything...*

*Me: Do you make it a habit of fucking with married men or did you make a special exception for my husband?* I waited for her response.

*Me: Hello?* No response.

*Me: Bitch, don't get quiet now!*

*ToiUwood1000: Your man made a special exception for me. I'm just that good.*

I know she didn't!

*Me: If you were that good you'd have him coming home to you every night.*

*ToiUwood1000: It's not over yet.*

*Me: It'll never happen.*

*ToiUwood1000: You should know by now to never say never. You have a great day. Take care.*

*Me: Fuck you! Stay the hell away from my husband.*

A message popped up indicating that she had logged out and my last message wouldn't be delivered until she logged back in. The fact that she logged off without receiving my response only further infuriated me. I had yet to get my thoughts together about my conversation with Toi when I heard the doorbell. I was so not in the mood for whoever it was or whatever they were selling. I chose to ignore it until the idiot pressed the button again.

"Coming," I yelled, walking to the door.

I swung the door open, then frowned at the tall, lanky mail carrier standing before me. He held a white box in his hands and looked as annoyed with me as I was with him.

"It won't fit in the box," he said, pushing his glasses up on the slope of his nose. I grabbed my box then politely sent him on his way, by slamming the door in his face.

The package was addressed to me. There wasn't a name on the return label, just the address of a post-office box. I pulled the clear strip of sealing tape back, then pulled open the flaps. Inside there was a pair of red lace thong panties. I pulled them out of the box while thinking if this was Carlton's way of making up with me, he had seriously lost some of his romantic game and I was not impressed. They weren't even my size! They were way too big. Then I looked at the garment again and noticed something that both disgusted and angered me. All over it was a white, crust-like substance that strangely resembled semen.

*****

"Have you seen these before?" I demanded, as soon as Carlton walked through the front door. I stood by the door holding the panties I received earlier with a pair of metal tongs. I planned to throw both of them in the trash as soon as I finished grilling my husband.

"What?" He asked, shutting the door behind him.

"Do you recognize these?" I repeated slowly.

"No," he said, staring at me like I had lost my damn mind. "Where is CJ?"

"In his room," I said. "Are you sure?"

"I'm positive," he said. "Why? Where did they come from?"

"Someone sent them to me this morning," I advised him. "No note, no nothing, but I think it was your little girlfriend."

"Who?" he asked, walking toward the spare bedroom.

"All of a sudden you got amnesia?" I asked, trailing behind him. "Toi! The same little tramp who sent me an IM talking mad trash."

"Toi doesn't know where we live," he yawned, removing his shirt. "And what do you mean, she instant messaged you?"

"Well, somebody sent them!" I vented. "They didn't just walk up and ship themselves!"

I wanted to scream out loud! It was obvious his tramp sent them and he looked completely unfazed. I tossed the tongs on the floor.

"And how you know she didn't follow you? Seriously, you don't know what she's capable of. She thought she was messaging you until I bust her ass. What in the hell were you thinking, Carlton? You told her where we live? Who does that?" I ranted, breathing heavily. "If you're going to be a cheater, Carlton, the least you can do is not be a stupid one!"

"I forget, you're the expert," he said sarcastically. He sat on the edge of the bed while taking off his shoes. I knew he was referring to my little rump with Lance.

"I guess forgive and forget only applies when you're the one who's wrong." I said, lowering my eyes.

"I was simply stating a fact," he said.

"Here's a fact for your ass," I said, frustrated. "She sent them. I know it's hard to believe, but keep in mind a lot of unbelievable things have been happening. Perfect example, I never *believed* you would cheat on me but we both know I was wrong."

I rolled my eyes at him then stepped out the room, slamming the door behind me. It was bad enough I had to listen to Toi with my man but now she was sending me physical evidence and it was obvious that Carlton didn't believe me! If she wasn't anything else she was bold, that's for sure, and she sure had him fooled. I marched back to my bedroom, then shut the door. Several minutes later I heard Carlton mumbling from the living room. I eased the bedroom door open slowly and stepped into the hall, only to realize he was on the phone.

"I told you," he said. "I don't give a damn. Stay away from my home and my family. After that shit you pulled, you're lucky I don't put my foot in your ass. You heard me. Get your emotions under control."

I came into the light of the living room where he could see me. Our eyes locked but neither one of us said a word. I smiled slightly, then went into the kitchen to start my husband's dinner. Maybe he did care.

# Chapter 18

## Toi

I was still pissed off about what had happened at my home. Granted, my renters' insurance had covered the cost of replacing the window, but I shouldn't have had to deal with it in the first place. Since the incident, I kept receiving hang-up calls from a blocked number. I finally broke down and changed my number. I didn't bother with trying to provide Carlton with the new one. The more I thought about it the more I asked myself was it all worth it? Now my answer was no. It was a week later when Carlton finally called me at the store and asked if he could come over. I immediately said no.

"Please, Toi," he begged. "I need to see you."

"I'm done, Carlton," I snapped. "I don't need the drama that comes along with you. Be a husband and father and leave me alone."

"Baby, please just let me talk to you face-to-face," he pleaded. "We can't let things end like this. Please, Toi."

I knew I should have said no, but instead I broke down and agreed to meet him. I told him that I wasn't comfortable meeting at my home so instead we opted to meet at a park.

"Is it possible that Lisa knows where I live?" I asked, as the two of us sat in his car.

"No. Why?"

"Someone threw a brick through my window," I said. "The same day you left the flowers on my doorstep."

He frowned. "What?"

"First the flowers were beautiful, thank you," I said appreciatively. "However, when I got them inside I discovered a snake."

"What?"

"Yes, it was only a little garden snake but it scared the hell out of me," I confessed. "The courtesy officer said that it probably slithered into the box to find shelter from the heat, but later I was in bed and the next thing I know, I hear a crash coming from the living room. As it turned out, someone threw a brick through it." He remained silent.

"When the officers arrived, we found the imprints of high heels," I continued.

"It was a woman," he concluded, shaking his head.

"Yep." I sighed. "One with big feet and a good-ass arm."

"You're thinking it was Lisa?"

"Yes," I said dramatically. "Who else would do such a thing?"

"I can truthfully say it wasn't Lisa," he said. "She was at home with me."

"Well, she must have a friend do her dirt for her."

"I don't think so," he said. "But I'll find out."

"This is just too much," I said frustrated.

"I'm sorry, Toi. Is that why you changed your number?" he asked. "To keep me from contacting you?"

"No, I did that because someone was playing on my phone," I said, getting pissed all over again. "My finger also points to your wife for that one."

"I don't know what to say," he said, looking at me with

sympathetic eyes. "I'll pay for the window but I know it wasn't her."

"It's not your fault," I said, exhaling. "My insurance covered it and to be honest, I just really want it to be over and put all the bs behind me."

"So you want us to be over?"

"I think it's best," I said.

"Toi…"

"Carlton, we need to just chill out," I said "Before things get out of hand and someone gets hurt more than they already have."

"Toi, I really care about you," he said, staring at me.

I was trying my hardest not to get caught up in his eyes and fall victim to his voice nor the throbbing in between my legs. "I'd better go," I said, opening the car door.

"Baby, just listen," he said, grabbing my arm gently.

"Carlton, let's just let it go." I pulled away, then climbed out the car and shut the door. In an instant he was out of the driver's side door and moving toward me.

"Toi, please," he said, stepping in front of me. "Just a little more time."

"Carlton…"

"Come on, baby," he said, lifting my chin with his finger. "Please."

I closed my eyes in an attempt to avoid his gaze and the temptation I was feeling to succumb to it. I sighed lightly while staring at him.

"Okay," I whispered.

Carlton smiled brightly before kissing my lips. I parted my lips allowing our tongues to engage themselves. He grabbed my breast gently through my blouse while backing me up against the passenger side door.

"Carlton," I moaned, pulling away. "We need to stop."

"Okay," he huffed, tracing kisses along my neck. He pulled me against his body then opened the car door before spinning me around to face the car. In what felt like an instant Carlton had my dress up around my hips.

"Spread your legs," he ordered,slipping his hand inside my panties. Carlton squeezed then tugged on my clit while tracing the curve of my ear with his tongue.

The park was empty and the spot we had chosen was hidden under the shadows of two large oak trees but the possibility of the two of us getting caught was still there, however, it didn't matter. There was a heated-storm brewing in between my legs that needed to be calmed and only one thing could bring an end to it's fury. I opened my legs allowing him to have full access to what he wanted. The cool air greeted my exposed kitten and bare ass when Carlton pulled my panties down around my ankles. I freed my left ankle from the restraint of my thongs allowing them to rest against my right heel. I reached behind me grabbing the wood pressing against the zipper of Carlton's uniform while shaking, as his fingers purged and explored inside me. The gushing sounds coming from in between my legs were evidence of just how wet he made me.

"Put your hands on the car," Carlton ordered, roughly. I obeyed. Leaning forward with both hands on the car, I waited impatiently while he freed his man, I shifted my weight on my right heel, bending my left leg up against the car window, granting him an open invitation. Carlton found his way into my heated center with passion-filled force and sexual aggression. The car rocked slightly as dove deep, pushing in and out then banging from wall to wall until finally reaching the eye of my storm.

# Chapter 19

## Toi

### Three months later

Carlton's lack of availability was beginning to get to me. I knew what I said but screw that, a woman is entitled to change her mind and mine was changed, I was no longer content with being the side chick and I needed some fulltime-available-all the-time love. Fifteen-minute quickies were not nor had they ever been my specialty, and I was fed up. The problem was that I was slightly addicted to Carlton and yes, I was sprung on the dick, even if I was only getting it for a quick nut. Another problem I had with breaking it off was that I loved the way I felt whenever I was around him and the way he brought out the vixen in me. The daring things we did and the inappropriate places we chose to do them were turn-ons in themselves. It wasn't like I could prevent it, the sexual chemistry between us was so strong that it made it extremely difficult for me to keep my hands off him.

I sat with my bare ass on the wooden table inside the stockroom and my back against the wall. The skirt of the dress I wore was pushed up around my waist while my lace panties dangled from my left thigh. I had one heel up on the table and the other resting over Carlton's shoulder as he played in between my parted thighs.

"Umm," I moaned, cupping his head with both hands. I ran my fingers across the soft waves caressing the top of his head.

Carlton held my lips open with his fingers while suckling gently on my clit. I was already wet and ready when I greeted him at the door; however, with the care and attention he was providing me I was now soaking, literally.

"Right there…right there…" I moaned, rotating my hips. The muscles in my stomach flinched involuntarily as my favorite warm-tingling sensation coursed through my core. "Damnit," I squealed with delight while opening my eyes.

"Satisfied?" he asked, standing up straight.

He licked his lips while staring at me with his brown eyes wide.

"Of course," I said, taking a deep breath. "Can't you tell?"

"Just making sure," he smiled, showing his dimples. He extended his hand to me, helping me down off the table. "I hate to eat and run…"

"Cute," I laughed, slipping my panties back on.

"But I'm officially late," he said.

I smoothed my hands down the front of my skirt, then extended my arms to him and gave him a tight squeeze.

"I'll call you before I leave the warehouse," he said, kissing the top of my head. "I want to see you later so I'm going to try and get out but if I don't…"

"I know…I know…" I sighed loudly. I wasn't going to pretend that I was the least bit happy about the 'maybe we will see each other' promise.

"What's wrong?"

"This isn't working," I explained. "I thought I would be cool with the occasional hook up, but I'm not.."

"What are you saying?" he asked.

"Maybe we should call this off," I said.

"Is that what you want?" he asked, staring at me.

"No, but I don't want things to be like this either," I said.

"Toi, just give me a little more time," he begged. "Please."

"I think you should go," I said, ignoring his request.

"Baby—"

"Just go."

He looked at me, then did as I requested, exiting the stockroom and then the front door.

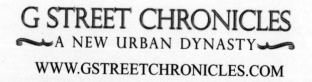

# Chapter 20

## Lisa

"I think you should go," Carlton advised me, as the two of us sat on the sofa holding hands. We were watching TV and discussing plans for the upcoming weekend; the weekend my youngest sister, Krissy, had chosen to say her "I Dos". I had planned to attend the wedding until Carlton advised me that he had committed to work at the last minute. Three months had passed since I overheard his little talk with Toi and since then, we had been back on good terms. I managed to move past his affair and look at the bigger picture; Carlton loved me and was with me. Plus, he hadn't given me any further reason to doubt him since. Still, I was skeptical about the two of us spending the weekend apart.

"I don't know," I said, exhaling. "I just thought this would be a great little getaway for us as a family."

"It would," he agreed. "But you know I'm trying to get a promotion and backing out of a commitment won't be a good look."

There was supervisor position that came open at A-Ex that Carlton was working hard to claim. The position would mean a significant pay increase, and it would also mean an office job; no more deliveries. It further meant a set schedule of 9 to 5.

"You're right," I said. "Maybe we'll plan a family vacation once you get your new job."

"Sounds good," he smiled, while squeezing my hand.

His cell phone rang, interrupting our talk.

"Gabe," he said, looking at the caller ID. "Hello. Yeah, what's up?…Okay," he said, looking at his watch. "Give me a minute. Yeah." He pressed the end button on his phone, then slid his hand from mine.

"His car won't start," he said, standing. "He needs me to come get him."

I looked at the clock and saw that it was a little after ten o'clock. "Where's he at?" I questioned.

"Over off Oakwood Avenue," he said, grabbing his keys off the coffee table.

"You want me to call AAA so they can send a tow truck?" I offered.

"It's probably just the battery again. No need in wasting money," he said, walking to the door. "It's been acting up the past week or so and knowing him, he hasn't bought a new one. I'll be back in a little bit. Okay?"

"Okay," I said, hesitantly. "Be careful."

"I will," he replied before walking out the door.

I wasn't feeling the fact that he was leaving the comfort of our home at what I considered to be an indecent hour to assist Gabe with something he as a man should have already taken care of, but I chose not to voice my opinion. As I said before, Carlton and I had been getting along well and although he had been working later more, I was happy with our progress.

Lately, Gabe had been calling and coming around more often for this, that, or whatever but it hadn't been an issue. In fact, it helped that Carlton wasn't going out, especially not with Robert. The only reason Gabe's calling was an issue for me now was because he interrupted my quality time with my husband. The two of us had a fun-filled evening, which included taking CJ to the movies and dinner, but I hoped that with CJ in bed, we could have some adult fun. I couldn't remember the last time we made love and although several times we had gone for days and even months without sex, this was the first time I actually couldn't remember him asking for some. I shrugged off my feelings of disappointment, then resumed watching TV.

After two hours and no sign of Carlton I began to get concerned, so much so that I picked up the phone and dialed his number.

"Hello," he answered. His voice was deep and low, the way it gets when he first wakes up.

"Where you at ?" I asked, annoyed.

"Over here...I dozed off," he said, groggy. "I'm on my way."

"Did y'all get the car fixed?" I questioned.

There was complete silence in the background. I wondered if Gabe had dozed off too or if there was more to the story.

"Yeah," he said, "I'm on my way."

"Okay—"

Carlton hung up before I could say anything else. My natural instinct was telling me that there was something not right about the situation. Various thoughts and scenarios began to run through my mind. *Had* Gabe called earlier? Could it have been another woman? My curiosity began to get the best of me. I logged onto my laptop and launched the Internet. A minute later I was signed into my Verizon account and scanning Carlton's activity for the current bill cycle. The numbers on the bill confirmed that it was Gabe who'd called earlier. In fact, there were no numbers on the bill that I hadn't seen before. After looking at his text usage, I concluded that I was looking for something that wasn't there. I shut down my laptop, then went into my bedroom where I slipped into one of my satin gowns and climbed into bed.

*****

The sound of the shower running awakened me. I stretched my arms above my head then rolled over onto my side to check the time. I had been sleeping for over an hour. I wondered how long Carlton had been home. I sat up against the headboard waiting for him to finish. The bathroom door opened and Carlton stepped out, followed by a billow of steam. He was completely naked with tiny droplets of water still covering his skin. I gazed at his body while thinking to myself how fine my husband was and how glad I was that he was all mine.

"You're up," he said, looking at me. "Did I wake you?"

"Yes, but it's cool," I said, yawning.

"Sorry about that," he said, walking over to our dresser. I watched as he picked up the bottle of lotion sitting on top of the dresser, then walked over and sat on the edge of the bed. He sat with his back facing me while rubbing lotion over his legs and feet.

"So what's was wrong with the car?" I asked, running my fingers through my hair.

"The battery."

"How did you manage to doze off?"

"We had a couple of beers," he said. "I guess I was more tired than I thought."

He spread lotion over his chest then finally his biceps before returning the bottle to the dresser.

"Are you still tired?" I asked

"A little bit," he said, pulling the sheets back and getting into bed.

"Well, maybe I can help you recover," I offered, while moving closer to him. I ran my hand over his pecs, down his washboard stomach, to his cock. His body tensed up instantly. I rubbed the head then shaft of his penis while trailing kisses along his chest. I noticed despite my continuous efforts, I received no response.

"You know," he said, grabbing my wrist gently. "Maybe we should just lay here."

"You lay there," I said. I slowly slid down the bed until my mouth was almost touching his penis. "Let mama take care of everything."

"It's cool," he said. He shifted on the bed, almost kneeing me in the forehead in the process. "Let's just lay here."

I stared at him while trying desperately to maintain the control I had learned to develop over the months. "Were you with her?" I asked calmly.

"Her who?"

"Toi," I said, disgusted. "Were you with her tonight?"

I sat up straight in bed while looking at him, waiting for an answer.

"I can promise you," he sighed. "I was not with Toi tonight."

I searched his eyes with mine. He was telling the truth, I could feel it. However, that didn't explain his lack of desire.

"Are you still attracted to me?" I asked.

I have always been confident when it came down to my looks and my body but in that moment, I started questioning the things I loved about me. Was I too thin? Too tall? Too pale? My physical insecurities were knocking at the door and I had given in and answered.

"You're very attractive," he said, sitting up then facing me.

"You know that."

"Then why is this happening?" I asked. "Did she do something that I don't?"

"No," he said, reassuringly. "I'm just tired. That's all."

"Okay," I said.

I eased back over to my side of the bed then stretched out on my side so that my back was facing him. I felt his hand on my shoulder.

"Come here," he ordered.

"Why?"

"Come here," he repeated.

I slid back into him, allowing him to wrap his arms around me. His arms were warm and strong like they've always been, but something felt terribly wrong and different to me.

# Chapter 21

## Lisa

When I graduated high school, I left my hometown of Chattanooga, Tennessee, with a duffel bag full of clothes, sixty dollars in my pocket, and a half a tank of gas. I had no clue what I was going to do or how I planned to get it done, but I did know that if I was ever going to have something in life, I was going to have to get out and go find it.

I always felt like I didn't belong, and that there was so much more in the world for me than the example that was set for me. Growing up I had more play uncles and cousins than most people have real ones. My mom went from bum to bum, leaping from one dead end relationship to another. Now my oldest sister, Monica, seemed content to follow in her footsteps. I, however, was determined to break the cycle. I'm not saying that I didn't have the occasional meaningless roll in the hay, or that I didn't have my own loose moments, but I liked to think I was a product of my environment.

After all, I lost my virginity at the tender age of 12 in the backseat of a Mustang convertible with my own mother cheering me on. However, I was always smart enough to know one of the real keys to financial stability was to get a good man who was willing to take care of me. The fact that my youngest sister Krissy was now tying the knot led me to believe she got the same message. Don't get me wrong, my mother may have been loose when it came to men, but she always made sure my sisters and I had food to eat and clothes on our backs. For those reasons alone, I held a certain amount of loyalty for her.

I sat in the plastic lawn chair watching my mother as she laughed hysterically while her latest boyfriend told degrading and sexist jokes. My mother stood in the midst of a crowd of about ten members of our family and a few of Krissy's and her fiancé Ken's friends. My mother wore a white halter dress and pink flip-flops, and had her arms wrapped around her male friend's neck, smiling like a schoolgirl. I didn't bother trying to remember his name because I was certain by the time I saw my mother again, he'd be replaced with the next man.

I frowned slightly while thinking how much I favored my mother: same blonde hair, straight nose, and blue eyes. The only difference was, my mother had developed bags under her eyes, and laugh lines. My sisters were both brunets with soft green eyes and pudgy noses. We always assumed they took after our father. Unfortunately for us, we never met the man—or men—to see if there was any stock in our claim. The one trait we all shared was our slim shapes. Even after childbirth, we could quickly drop back down to a size 6 or so with little effort.

"Be careful, CJ," I called out to my son. I watched him as he and Monica's 2 and 6 year-old sons chased one another across the lawn.

"CJ is looking more and more like his daddy," Monica said. She sat reclining in the chair opposite of me, with her legs spread, wearing a pair of denim short-shorts and a red tank top. Krissy and Ken sat to her left, sharing a chair and appearing to be in a world of their own.

"Speaking of his daddy, how is he?" She flashed her green eyes at me and smiled. My sister liked to get under my skin and she did so easily.

"Carlton is fine," I said, flatly.

"Don't I know it," she laughed, smacking her lips. "Tell him I send my love."

I cut my eyes at her. My sister had no problem letting me know that she would get with Carlton if given the opportunity. Monica was not only a slut but a disloyal slut. If you had something she wanted and she could get it, she would use her power—and by power I meant pussy—to get it. I shot her a glare that said, *watch yourself, bitch.*

"Monica, leave her alone," Krissy chimed in. "You know how she gets."

Krissy was referring to my temper when it came down to my husband. In the past when Monica made an inappropriate comment, I'd been known to snap. I still had it in me, but I knew the weekend wasn't about me and I didn't want to ruin Krissy's moment. In an effort to keep the peace, I chose to keep any additional comments to myself.

"I'll be back," I said, standing with my phone in hand. I stepped away from the crowd while pressing 1 on my speed dial. The phone rang several times until I finally hung up. I figured Carlton was still working and unable to get to his phone.

*****

I pressed the end button on my cell phone while staring at my watch. It was 2:00 am in Chattanooga, which meant it was 1:00 am in Huntsville. I had been trying to reach Carlton for the last hour to no avail. *Where is he? I thought.* I tried his cell phone again and once again it went directly to voice mail. I pressed the end button on my phone. then dropped it back in my handbag. I promised myself I wouldn't freak out.

"Are you still trying to call him?" my sister Krissy asked, coming up behind me. She carried a half-empty Budweiser bottle in her hands. She stepped in front of me, standing with her legs spread, causing the red spandex mini-dress she wore to creep even further up her legs. Looking at her dress made me suddenly self-conscious of my own attire. I had borrowed a fitted, sleeveless red lamé dress from Krissy for the night. The dress was moderate compared to the matching dresses that she and Monica had on, but it too was a thread away from showing my ass. Before Carlton and I started dating the dress, along with several other pieces of lingerie I passed off as dresses, would have been welcomed in my closet. Now I chose to wear things that my husband would be proud of. I knew he wouldn't approve of my attire but like Monica reminded me, he wasn't there and it was only for one night. Besides, I was not going to be outdone by my sisters, especially not Monica.

I had chosen to join Krissy, Monica, and Krissy's two best friends for a bachelorette party in Krissy's honor. The party started at a local bar and pub and now the three of us planned to continue the party at Club Foxtails, a strip club just outside the city. Krissy's friends chose not to join us at the strip club. I was against the extra stop too but agreed again for the sake of keeping the peace between me and my sisters. Besides, your baby sister only gets married once—if she's lucky.

Krissy rocked slightly as she stared at me. She was on what I counted to be her third beer, beers that she had used to chase straight shots of Jack Daniels.

"Yes," I answered, stating the obvious.

She shook her head, causing her shoulder-length brown hair to swing back and forth. "You need to get some control over your shit," she said, smacking her lips. "That's what's wrong with you. You don't have no control…you've been with that man so long that he is now calling all the shots…"

I was not in the mood to discuss my marriage and control with someone who wasn't married her damn self yet, and who appeared to be a sneeze away from being pissy drunk.

"Whatever," I said, defensively. "I got mine under control, you just make sure you can handle yours."

"Bitch, Ken know," she said, putting her hands on her hips. "He know who, what, when, and where!"

"Krissy and Lisa, let's go!" Monica yelled. She stood by the club entrance, looking in our direction.

"I can't stand that slut," Krissy slurred, pulling me by the hand.

"Me neither," I said honestly. "Me neither."

Inside the club, we were greeted by a tall redhead with big brown eyes. She stood towering over us in silver platforms with six-inch heels, red boy shorts, and a red bikini top that barely covered her nipples.

"Welcome to Foxtails, ladies." She smiled while checking our IDs one by one. "Enjoy."

I hadn't been to the club since my last trip home, which was a little over a year ago, and it was clear there had been renovations. At that time the club only had one stage, a bar, and a deejay booth. There was now another stage to the left once you passed the greeter, and one directly in the center of the room, surrounded by tables. The bar was still located to the right of the entrance and the DJ booth was still located in the far left corner. Monica explained there was now an adjacent pool hall that was added last year.

I followed my sisters through the crowd as they approached the seating area by the stage. Before we reached the seats a short, bald man with olive-colored skin grabbed Krissy's arm and pulled her toward him. The man wore jeans, a plaid, button-down shirt and looked old enough to be all of our fathers.

"Hey, baby," she grinned, throwing her arms around the man's neck.

"Krissy," I called, concerned about her inebriated condition.

"She's fine," Monica said. "That's JD…he's a friend. Come on."

I looked back at Krissy and the man and saw the two of them with their arms and hands all over each other like lovers. It was obvious her pending nuptials didn't mean a thing. I decided not to concern myself with what they were doing, and to try my best and have a good time despite having Monica as my company.

Monica and I found an empty table directly by the stage and sat down. A few minutes later a petite, dark-skinned woman wearing shorts and a bikini top identical to what the greeter wore came over. She introduced herself as Tina, then asked what she could get us.

"One Jack and Coke and one Jack straight," Monica ordered for us both. I hadn't drank whiskey in years. I was now more of a vodka girl but I figured if Monica was paying I would roll with the punches. I knew with the music blasting in the club I wouldn't be able to hear my phone, so I placed it on vibrate before sitting it on top of the table. I wanted to be prepared in the event that Carlton called.

"Girl, put that phone up," Monica said loudly. "We are here to have a good time, not to play check-in with a damn man." I ignored her and left my phone where it was. She rolled her eyes, then directed her attention to the female on stage.

The woman moved and rolled her wide hips while leaning against the shining metal pole and mouthing the words to Ciara's song, "Ride." She had long, jet-black hair that hung at her waist, and dark-chocolate colored, flawless skin that glimmered under the light. She wore nothing but heels and bikini bottoms that left very little to the imagination. Once Tina returned with our drinks, Monica paid her, then requested change before redirecting her attention back to the stage.

"Whoo hoo!" She yelled, waving her hands in the air. She held up three, crisp one-dollar bills, then stood waiting on the dancer. The woman smiled as she eased down to the floor and crawled seductively over to the edge of the stage. She rolled her hips back and forth in front of Monica while squeezing her full, dark nipples. She flicked her tongue out while cupping her large breasts, then slowly traced the tip around her left areola, then her right before sitting on the edge of the stage with her legs spread. She motioned with one finger, beckoning Monica.

Monica happily obliged. I watched as the dancer wrapped her long legs around Monica's waist and began to grind against her wildly. She leaned back onto the stage, pulling Monica up on the stage until she was straddling her waist. The short blue dress Monica had on inched up revealing her black lace thongs. The dancer grabbed Monica by the waist as she mimicked riding her. The men and some of the women surrounding the stage began to cheer them on. I felt like I was watching the two of them in bed as the dancer ran her hands up and down Monica's behind before pulling her dress up until her butt was completely exposed.

Monica continued to grind against her, while the woman

slapped then squeezed her bare cheeks. By the time the song went off Monica's face was flushed and the dancer needed assistance picking up her tips before the next dancer hit the stage. I sipped my drink slowly while shaking my head. My sister still loved being the life of the party.

"Girl, she is fine," she laughed, returning to her chair. "And her legs are strong as hell."

"So I see," I said.

She tossed back her drink, then laughed and said, "That was the PG version."

"Then you need to take it to G," I said.

"Whatever," she said, smacking her lips. "I don't have a husband." She held up her left hand. "See, no rings on this finger."

*Keep acting like that in public and you'll never get one*, I thought.

"To each her own," I said, before taking another sip of my drink.

"Don't play with it," Monica egged. "Take it to the head."

"Moderation," I said.

"Geez," she exhaled dramatically. "Why do you always have to be a stick in the ass?"

"I'm not," I said.

"Whatever," she laughed. "You are such a prude now."

"I'm happy," I told her. "My life is good."

"If you say so," she said. "But a bore in public usually means a bore in bed. You sure Carlton is satisfied?" She grinned while staring at me mischievously. "You know I can give you some pointers or help you out if you want me to."

"Fuck you, bitch," I snapped, angrily.

Monica's face lit up as she began to smile brightly. "That's incest," she said, before blowing me a kiss.

"Go to hell," I said. I grabbed my phone and purse then

eased off my chair.

"Oh come on, Lisa!" she yelled behind me. "I'm just joking with you."

I looked at my phone, making sure I hadn't missed a call or message from Carlton while marching away from Monica. *Nothing.*I dropped my phone in my purse while stepping down into the pool hall. The room had four high chairs and tables lined along the wall and six pool tables scattered throughout. I sat down at one of the tables and sighed. A minute later Monica appeared carrying two glasses in her hand.

"Lisa," she said, sitting one of the glasses down in front of me.

"Leave me alone, Monica," I said, cutting my eyes at her.

"Look I'm sorry," she said, seriously. "I shouldn't have gone there. I know how you feel about that and I was wrong. I don't want to fight with you tonight. K?"

I stared in her green eyes. She actually looked sincere about her apology.

"Come on," she said raising her glass. "Cheers."

I inhaled deeply then blew the air out slowly through my parted lips.

"Come on, Lisa."

I rolled my eyes then raised my glass. I had a love-hate relationship with Monica but the fact remained she was still my big sister.

"Cheers," she smiled.

"Whatever, wench," I mumbled.

"Skank," she said, tapping her glass against mine lightly. We both laughed before turning our glasses up .

Fifteen minutes later Krissy staggered in the pool hall with JD and informed us he was going to drop her off at Mom's house.

By that time I was feeling so good she could have told me she was being airlifted by aliens and I wouldn't have given a damn.

"Love you ," Krissy said, before turning to leave.

"I can't believe she's tying the knot," I said, shaking my head.

"Just another damn day," Monica said, tossing her hair over her shoulders.

I laughed.

"Do you see yourself ever getting married?" I asked her.

"For what?" she laughed. "To keep doing the shit I'm doing now? No, thank you."

"Um, you may actually end up loving the man," I said.

"If I love him I don't have the heart to fuck 'em over," she said, seriously. "Why you think I let Zack go?"

Zack was the father of Monica's children. They had been heavily involved up until the birth of their youngest son, when Monica broke things off. I liked Zack. He was not only a good father to my nephews but Monica admitted he was good to her.

"Why did you?"

"Because he wanted the rings and the house with the little fence all that goody-goody shit," she frowned, waving her hand. "And he deserved it."

"And you don't?" I refused to believe that my sister was content being single.

"I did want it," she said. "But I would have gotten all of it and screwed it up before the ink dried on the marriage certificate. Zack didn't deserve that and I was woman enough to see it."

"How do you know if you didn't even try?"

"Because I'm my mama's daughter." Monica shrugged. "Like mama, I take something beautiful and mess it up…and if I don't mess it up the shit is corrupt from the beginning… It's just in our blood. We pick effed-up situations and we make them worse."

"Well, Carlton and I are happy," I said, stretching the truth.

"Are you?" she questioned. "Calling every hour on the hour… constantly checking your phone to see if he called?" She laughed while shaking her head. "Not to mention when you bring him around, you're on his ass like the scent of a fart! And that's just the shit that you've shown me. I can only imagine what you're not telling me. You're only sweating that man for one of two reasons, because you fucked up or because you know he will."

"Whatever," I said, rolling my eyes.

"You can deny it all you want," she said, leaning in close to me. "The truth is the truth. We all have issues. I was just the one real enough to own up to it."

The dancer she had been onstage with earlier entered the room, then motioned Monica to come to her. She climbed off her chair and kissed me on the cheek. "I'll be back." She smiled. I watched her as she wobbled off. I looked at my phone again while Monica's words replayed in my head.

# Chapter 22

## Lisa

Carlton provided me an early morning wake-up call, explaining that after he got off work he had a couple of beers and dozed off. There was something in his voice that wasn't quite right. Something that sent my radar up. When I questioned him about it, he stated that he was just tired.

"I better get ready for work," he said quickly. "I'm putting in another 12 hours today, but I'll call you when I get off."

"Talk to you then," I said.

"Kiss CJ for me," he said. "And tell him I love him."

"Will do," I said. "I love you."

"You too," he told me.

I hung up with a disturbing feeling that something was wrong. I decided not to focus on my feeling and instead to focus on my sister and the celebration of her big day.

That evening Krissy and Ken recited their vows in the outdoor garden of the Mountain Oaks wedding chapel, surrounded by hundreds of tiny white lights and red roses. To my surprise, Krissy's wedding and her choice of dress were very tasteful and elegant. I had to give credit where it was due; my sister looked stunning in her white, strapless fitted gown. She appeared to glow. The ceremony was simple and sweet. There were only about fifty guests in attendance, one of whom happened to be JD, but it was still nice. I noticed as she was walking down the aisle that she looked over at JD and casually winked. I was almost certain Ken saw her but then I noticed him checking out Krissy's maid of honor. Dysfunctional as my family may be they were still mine, and I was happy I'd taken the time to be with them.

I had just finished taking pictures with my sister and her new groom when I felt my phone vibrating in my handbag. I pulled out the device and saw that I had a text message.

*256-555-9666: The Westin Room 604*

*Me: Who is this?* The number looked somewhat familiar but I couldn't place it. Something inside of me told me to reply.

*256-555-9666: Is this Lisa?*

*Me: Yes*

*256-555-9666: You have a surprise waiting. The Westin Room 604.*

*Me: What's waiting?*

I waited impatiently for a reponse. After a minute I received my answer.

*256-555-9666: YOUR HUSBAND*

I waited several minutes after staring at the text messages before finally calling the number.

"Hello"

"Who is this?" I asked the female on the other end.

"This is Nesha"

# Chapter 23

## Toi

After enjoying dinner at the Watercress my palette was satisfied and my stomach was full. I now stared out the floor-to-ceiling glass window on the sixth floor of the Westin, admiring the view of the city lights below. Together, the white lights against the night sky created a stunning, intimate portrait. I had officially declared the Westin my favorite hotel, and with good reason; from the wood and marble accents throughout the room, right down to the feather-filled pillows covering the king-size bed, everything was perfect. Carlton contributed to the perfection by adding his own personal touches: covering the bed and floor with fresh rose petals; lining the bathroom counter with tea light candles; and welcoming me with an icy cold bottle of coconut CÎROC. When I asked how he'd managed to pull off all of it, he advised me that a little angel by the name of Nesha helped him. I made a mental note to thank her the next time I saw her.

When she called me earlier inviting me to dinner, I felt something wasn't right but I figured why not. It was Saturday night and my besties were both out on dates, Anitra with her husband and LaShay with a new guy she met at work. That left me alone and bored. When I arrived at the restaurant and saw Carlton I knew I had been set up and wanted no parts of their plan. It took a little persuasion on his part to get me to stay but I finally broke down and decided to give him a little of my time. As frustrated as I was with our situation, I still couldn't—or better yet, I refused to—resist his charm and the fact that I had been missing him.

"What are you doing?" Carlton asked.

He came up behind me and wrapped his arms around my waist. I leaned back against his chest, allowing my head to rest lightly against his shoulder.

"Enjoying the view," I answered.

"It's nice," he said, kissing the top of my head.

"Beautiful," I corrected him.

"Nope," he said. "It's nice. You're beautiful."

I turned on my heels so that the two of us were now standing and staring eye to eye. I wrapped my arms around his neck, interlocking my fingers behind his head. I smiled, appreciative of his compliment, then leaned in pressing my lips to his.

"Mmmm," I moaned, pressing my breasts against his chest.

"Be good," he said, pulling away.

"Why?" I asked, lowering my eyes. "Don't you like it when I'm bad?"

Carlton licked his lips while pulling my arms down from around his neck. He locked his fingers with those of my left hand while guiding my right hand to his crotch. He kept his eyes engaged with mine as he pressed my palm against the hardness buldging in his pants.

"Does that answer your question?" he asked.

"It does," I whispered, squeezing gently.

"Keep it up and you're going to be in trouble," he warned me.

"I like trouble," I mumbled, before kissing him again. I sucked on the tip of his tongue softly while continuing to massage him.

"I warned you," he said, easing me up against the window.

He trailed kisses from my earlobe down my neck while pulling up my knit dress until my Victoria's Secrets were exposed. I spread my legs, allowing him entrance to my moist playground while unbuckling his belt. He pulled my panties to the side with one hand while invading my warm territory with the other. I shivered as Carlton pushed his index finger in and out of my kitten slowly.

I quickly unbuttoned then unzipped his pants, giving myself enough room to reach over the elastic waistband of his boxers and cuff his hard joystick. I freed his man of the restraints of his clothing then slowly moved my hand up and down, beating him softly. He pulled his fingers from in between my legs then turned me around so that I was now facing the window. I spread my legs shoulder width apart as I waited anxiously. I could hear the clank of his belt as his pants fell around his ankles, the tearing of the wrapper as he opened the condom, and finally I felt his strength as he entered me from behind. I leaned forward, pressing both my palms against the clear glass, arching my back as I bounced toward him, taking every inch of his rock-hard dick.

*****

"Do you know how much I think about you?" Carlton asked, rubbing my back slowly.

The two of us lay in bed with our arms wrapped around each other. I traced my fingers up and around the curve of his chest while laying with my head on his stomach.

"No, but you should tell me," I said, kissing his navel.

"Much more than I ever expected I would." He said. "All the time."

"I think about you too," I confessed.

"Do you ever ask yourself what if?"

"What do you mean?"

"Like what if the two of us had met each other first?" he questioned.

"I try not to," I said, propping myself up on my elbows. "Why torture myself with something that can't be undone." He nodded in agreement.

"Well I guess I torture myself daily," he said, tracing the curve of my nose with his finger. "It's like sometimes I think I'm silently wishing or hoping for the shit to hit the fan."

# Chapter 24

## Lisa

When Nesha advised me of whom I was speaking to, I immediately hung up assuming the text messages were some little cruel, ignorant joke that Carlton and his friend were playing just to get me revved up, but that didn't stop me from making the two and a half hour drive back to Huntsville. When I arrived I dropped CJ off at my aunt's, then proceeded straight to the Westin. I now stood counting the illuminating numbers above the elevator door as I rode from the lobby toward the sixth floor. I could hear my heart pounding in my ears as I pictured what I was going to find once I reached room 604.

It could be a joke, I reminded myself. I could get there and be totally humiliated if Carlton wasn't, or I could get there and he could have something beautiful planned for me. I attempted to reason with myself as the elevator doors slowly opened. None of that mattered as I stepped across the carpeted floor checking the wooden numbers as I passed each door. I came to room number 604 then knocked lightly. I could hear the TV playing on the other side of the door but no voices. I waited then knocked again this time, I knocked harder.

"Coming." I heard a woman state from inside the room.

I could feel and practically taste the adrenaline flowing through my veins as I envisioned what was waiting on the other side of the door. When the door opened my eyes locked with those of a dark-skinned woman with big brown eyes and shoulder length, jet black hair. She stood at the door wearing a fitted T-shirt and boy shorts. She was barefoot and her face showed no signs of makeup. She looked like she had been relaxing before I disturbed her. *It is a joke*, I thought.

"Can I help you?" she asked, with raised eyebrows.

"I'm sorry —I—"

"Lisa."

Carlton's voice floated up from behind me. I spun on my heels to look at him. He stood staring at me like a possum stuck in the bright lights of a F250. He wore a gray T-shirt with gray basketball shorts and flip-flops. He held an ice bucket in his hands, filled to the brim with cubes. My eyes darted from his physique then back to his eyes again. The evidence of guilt floated through his corneas, screaming at me. I looked back at the woman. She stared me in my eyes, answering my question without so much as parting her lips. I had forgotten her voice but I sure as hell remembered the slut's name.

"Toi," I said lowly.

She dropped her eyes from mine momentarily, looked at him, then said, "Yes."

It's amazing how, when we're focused on what could be waiting for us, we tend to miss obvious signs and clues in our surroundings. From where I stood I could see the foot of the bed, the disheveled covers, my husband's overnight bag sitting on the floor by the built-in refrigerator, and the open box of Trojans laying on the counter. I hadn't noticed them before but now that my anger was coursing through my body, I noticed it all. My breath felt like it was stuck in my throat, strangling my esophagus. My heart felt as if it had dropped down to my French pedicure.

My hand felt like it took flight on wings, gliding through the air, as I turned, slapping Carlton hard across his face. I watched as the bucket slipped from his hands and ice fell around my ankles like chards of broken glass as he stumbled back. The sound of the impact cut through the air, breaking the tension-filled silence, while my hand throbbed fiercely.

"You lying piece of shit!" I snapped. My chest rose and fell roughly with every breath I took. I stared at him, waiting for him to do something, say anything. His eyes lowered to slits but he did nothing. I turned to face his tramp.

"I told you to stay away from my husband," I breathed. "You really should have listened." I cut my eyes at her before turning on my heels and pushing past Carlton.

"Don't bother coming home tonight," I warned him.

As I stepped on the elevator I held my head high, refusing to let them see the inner pain that was trying to push through past my anger.

*****

I hadn't touched a cigarette since high school but I felt under the circumstances, I was allowed a fix. I sat at my kitchen table with the lit Newport 100 sitting between my fingers and a half empty glass of Crown Royal in my other hand when there was a knock at the front door. I took a long drag then exhaled. If it was Carlton, he was better off staying away from me. There was no telling what I might do in my current state. I took long sip from my glass, flinching as the warm liquid burned a path down my throat.

The bell continued to chime until I couldn't take anymore. I tossed back the remaining contents in my glass, then put the cigarette out in it before pushing away from the table. I swung the door open, prepared to knock the taste from Carlton's lips again and instead found Gabe standing on my doorstep dressed in a light linen shirt and matching pants. He looked at me curiously.

"Did I catch you at a bad time?" he asked, standing with his hands cuffed in front of him.

"Carlton isn't here," I said, disregarding his question.

"I didn't come to see Carlton," he said lowly. "I came to see you. May I come in?"

"Why?"

"I know about my friend's error," he stated shaking his head. "I don't like the path he has chosen."

It was obvious what he meant was that he knew Carlton was screwing around on me and with my lack of patience at that moment, I really wished he would have just said that. I stepped back from the door, allowing him to enter. Gabe looked around, scanning my living room.

"I can see that I caught you at an uncomfortable moment," he said, walking over to the table. He picked up the near empty pint of liquor I had sitting on the table. "You know this is not the best way to deal with your troubles."

"Maybe not," I said, plopping down on the couch. "However, screwing another woman isn't either but your friend did. In fact he still is."

"Yes, Toi is a problem," he said, rubbing his hand across his chin. "A beautiful one but a problem no less."

"You've met her?"

"Yes, we had a small gathering at my residence a few months

ago and she was in attendance with Carlton."

"Who else was there?" I questioned.

"Quinton and Nesha."

"Perfect. So everyone knew except me," I said, shaking my head. I knew that all of them were Carlton's friends, but it didn't make me feel any less like a fool.

"Loyalty and confidentiality are one and the same," Gabe said, walking over to sit down next to me. "Carlton has earned that."

I rolled my eyes.

"However, he has not earned the right to play with the emotions of two, if I must say so myself, exquisite women." He licked his lips while looking at me. I suddenly felt underdressed in the maxi dress I had on.

"Is that why Nesha texted me?" I asked, "She's loyal to Carlton because of their friendship but she too disagrees with his decisions?"

"Could be," he said. "Who understands the thoughts of a woman?" He laughed. "Lord knows I've never been able to."

"Well, he's been getting away with it all this time and no one said anything," I said, shaking my head.

"Yes," he sighed. "But I think it's time for this little rendezvous with Toi to come to an end."

"Meaning?"

"Carlton's presence is needed here, not in some hotel spoiling another woman," he said. "He should be here taking care of the finer things that he seems to have forgotten he possess." He reached out and stroked my hair softly. "That is, if you want him here."

There was something in his eyes that told me that the conversation was no longer just about Carlton and Toi.

"Of course I want him here," I said. "Why wouldn't I? I love him."

He looked at me then nodded his head. "I just want you to know you also have your options."

"Thanks, but right now my option is getting my husband back to who he used to be."

"I can help you with that," he said, taking my hand in his. "In fact I have a suggestion."

"I'm listening..."

*****

After Gabe left I took a long hot shower, then slipped on my gown. Despite my better judgment, I took Gabe's advice, and called Carlton demanding that he come home so that we could talk right then. I was sitting on the sofa when the door to my home slowly opened. Carlton stepped inside, almost tripping over the bags I had sitting by the door. I should have had a hundred words for him as he stared at me, but only one made the escape from my throat.

"Go," I said, strongly. He looked from the bags to me. "Those are yours," I told him.

"Do you want to talk about this?" he asked. He stepped around his luggage, moving toward me.

"No," I said firmly. "I want you to go out there and find out what it is about her that you can't get enough of. And once you get yourself together, then and only then can you come back." I knew my words were not what he expected, but I meant every one of them. Gabe was right. It wasn't right for Carlton to live two lives in one world. It was time for him to let go of her and if that meant I had to let him go at that moment then so be it.

"Lisa—"

"I mean it," I said, throwing up my hand. "Don't come back until you've gotten yourself together."

He looked at me, gauging my expression then finally picking up the bags. "I'm sorry," he said, sadly.

I turned my head while fighting back my tears. I managed to keep them under wraps until he finally exited back out the door. As my tears overflowed freely I told myself that Gabe was right and this would work.

# CHAPTER 25

## Toi

I hated the way things played out at the hotel but there was no way for any of us to turn back the hands of time. When Carlton saw Lisa standing at the door, I could have sworn I saw something that closely resembled relief. For a brief moment I asked myself if he had anything to do with Lisa mysteriously discovering where we were. After listening to him apologize for putting me in such a terrible position, I concluded he had nothing to do with it.

When Carlton told me that he was not going back I *was* relieved, not only because of my feelings for Carlton but because it was evident that their relationship was toxic. I was hoping that this was what the two of them needed to finally go their separate ways and move on. Seriously, how many times do two people have to hurt each other until they finally come to the realization that they're not meant to be together?

"I'll see you when you get off," Carlton smiled.

The two of us stood in the parking lot of my apartment embracing. He was headed off to work and I was headed back to bed for another two to three hours before I had to go in myself.

"Have a good day," I said, sweetly.

"You too, beautiful."

I wrapped my arms around his neck, pulling him down to eye level with me. I gave him a tender kiss on the lips before pulling away and heading back to my apartment. I climbed back in bed then curled up with my pillow. As soon as I closed my eyes, my home phone began to ring. I didn't recognize the number but I answered anyway.

"Hello?"

"Did I wake you?" A female voice asked. She spoke politely like the two of us were friends.

"Um, not really," I said, sitting up in bed. "Who is this?"

"This is Lisa," she said.

"Lisa?"

"Yep…Good morning," she said politely.

"Good morning." I said, dazed and slightly confused.

"May I speak to Carlton?"

"Carlton's not here." I informed her.

"What time will he be home?" she asked.

It was obvious that Lisa thought Carlton and I were now living together. He had spent the night with me; however, his plan was to get his own apartment as soon as possible. Until then he had taken residence with Robert again.

"Carlton doesn't live here," I informed her. "So I'm not sure what time he'll be home or how you got this number."

"But he was there last night," she stated firmly, ignoring my statement about how she got my number.

"You shouldn't make assumptions," I said. "Just because he's not there with you doesn't mean he's here with me."

"So it's just my imagination?" She asked. "He wasn't there?"

"No," I lied. I was trying not to make things worse for Carlton.

"Okay! Good," she said, sounding like she was smiling. "Well, have a wonderful day. Talk to you soon."

I stared at the phone after she ended our call, while pondering over how strange the phone call had been and asking myself, what exactly did she mean by *talk to you soon*?

*****

I was so busy attempting to merchandise my store in preparation of an upcoming visit from my district manager, that I didn't have time to accomplish anything else, so much so that I was practically doing kicks when 1:00 pm came and Chloe came in to relieve me. Once she arrived, I decided to take a quick lunch break and grab something to eat.

I was sitting in the drinking room of Tellini's when my phone chimed, notifying me that I had an e-mail. I had received a notification earlier but I had ignored it. I tapped on the mail icon and waited for my messages to come up. I saw that I had notifications from Facebook indicating I had comments on a picture I posted. I found this odd because one, I hadn't posted on Facebook in weeks and two, I had chosen not to receive notifications on my phone. I opened the e-mail and saw that there was a thread of comments. The first one was from a user by the name of Bob Babylikesthedick Jones and it read "Bitch, I got that work for you!!" I scrolled down and saw the majority of the replies were much on the same level, sexually explicit.

"What the hell?" I said, while shaking my head at some of the comments. There were comments from women and men stating what they would do to me or what I could suck or lick. There were others calling me a hoe, slut, triflin' bitch, and other derogatory terms.

I clicked on "Go to comments" so I could view the photo

they were commenting on and almost pissed on myself when I saw the photo was of me sitting with my legs spread open, wearing nothing but my bikini. The picture had been posted on a page titled Hoe for Hire. The caption at the bottom of the photo read: "I give discounts." The photo was one I had taken and sent to Carlton weeks ago. I knew without a doubt he would never share it with anyone else.

That left one person and one person only, Lisa. It was obvious she had gained access to the picture through his phone. I quickly got my food boxed to go, then hurried back to the store so that I could pull up my page on the store laptop. By the time I logged in from work, the picture had been shared eight times and had 30 more comments added to the original 100. It was then that I discovered the photo stated it had been posted by me, which meant one thing: my account had been hacked.

I quickly deleted the picture from the original page, then went to the shares to see if I could do the same. When I discovered I couldn't, I screamed with anger. I changed my password on Facebook, then went to my e-mail and did the same thing. After that I went to every page that showed my photo had been shared and opted to report the image. It didn't matter by that time; it had probably already been viewed by thousands. I remembered Carlton telling me the name of the salon where Lisa worked. I googled the number then called with the hope that Lisa would answer.

"Thank you for calling Ellen's, this is Lisa."

"You hacked my account," I said, accusingly.

"Toi," she said. "What a pleasant surprise…Hold on just a second."

I heard her speaking to someone in the background then the sound of a register. "Have a nice day, see you next time." I could hear the sound of a door chiming. It was obvious she was at work. "Ellen, I'll be back," she said. "I'm going to take me a quick break." I listened to the sound of her heels clicking as she walked.

"Thank you for holding," she said, "Unfortunately, due to unforeseen circumstances I have to work more than I did before. That leaves me very little time to talk so let's make this quick. Now what can I help you with?"

*This bitch is crazy!* I thought to myself.

"You don't have time to talk but you sure as hell found time to hack my Facebook account," I blasted. "You posted the picture I took for Carlton and I want you to know I'm pressing charges." I knew legally my only option was a possible civil suit against her, but I was angry and attempting to instill fear.

"No, I didn't hack your account," she said, innocently. "I would never do that!" She took a deep breath then exhaled. "Because, I don't know how…So someone had to do it for me." She laughed sadistically. "And you can threaten to press charges all you want, boo boo, we both know even if I did do it, you can't prove it."

She had a valid point. I couldn't prove it and that alone made me furious.

"That's what your ass gets for taking pics for the next woman's man. Not what you had planned for that little photo. Huh?" She laughed again then sighed.

"Your husband can't get enough of me. Not what you had planned for your marriage. Huh?" I asked, heated. *Silence.* "Who's laughing now, bitch," I added. She hung up. I ran my fingers through my hair while silently cursing her again.

My cell phone began to ring. It's probably her calling back, I thought. If Lisa wanted a war of words I was prepared to give her one. Hell, at that point I was ready to whoop her ass, in fact I would say I owed her an ass whooping. I looked at the caller ID and saw that it was my mother calling. I exhaled loudly. I loved my mother but whenever she called it was for one or two things: to ask me what I'd been learning at church or to remind me that I was not getting any younger and I needed a husband. I contemplated on letting her go to voice mail but decided against it.

"Hey mama," I answered.

"Toi LeAnna Underwood!" she screamed from the other end.

The use of my full name was a clear indication that my mother was pissed about something.

"Yes?" I asked, annoyed. My mother was a drama queen in every sense of the word. I couldn't understand for the life of me how she managed to get my father. He was a quiet, meek man who I had never heard raise his voice. Mama on the other hand felt the need to turn a rainy day into a natural disaster.

"What are you doing over there?" she shrieked. "Pastor McCaulley called me and first he stated that you haven't been in attendance in months…"

Pastor McCaulley was my church pastor and good friends with my mother. After she and my father chose to relocate to Houston, Pastor McCaulley became somewhat of my mother's church spy. I was brought up attending church service regularly and even after my parents departure, I continued to attend services every Sunday. Lately though, my attendance had simmered down to once a month. If I went at all. It wasn't that my faith had faltered, I just was no longer feeling that particular church or its judgmental members, especially considering the way I now chose to live my life.

"*Then* he advised me that there are pictures of you half naked floating around on some Facebook sex page!" She continued. "What is wrong with you? Are you on drugs!"

I was speechless as she ranted and raved about the photo she admitted she hadn't seen herself but that the pastor described as sinful.

"Why would you do such a thing?" she asked. "Toi, I taught you better than that! Posting indecent photos is not Godly! That is not how you get a man! You're supposed to pray, little girl. Have you forgotten how to do that? You better hope your father doesn't find out about this! Hello…hello?"

"First of all, I didn't post the picture," I informed her. My voice, much like my blood pressure, was elevated. My mother hadn't attempted to ask me my side of the story. She called and instantly jumped to conclusions. "It just looks like I did because my Facebook account was hacked. Second, what is the pastor doing looking at adult pages anyway?"

"That has nothing to do with the fact that you're on there!" She sounded slightly offended. "The pastor is trying to save lost souls by any means necessary! Besides he says you were wearing your bra and panties with your legs gapped open," she continued. "Why would you be posing like that in the first place?"

"Because I'm grown and I wanted to," I advised her. "I took that picture for my friend and I was wearing a bathing suit, not my bra and panties."

"What's the difference? And your so-called friend shared it with the world," she retaliated. "And who is this friend? And why haven't I heard of him until now?"

"He didn't share anything with anyone," I said sarcastically. "His *wife* did and that's why you haven't heard of him, mama, because he's married and frankly I didn't want to deal with your unsolicited opinions on who I choose to date. So go ahead and add that to the long list of ungodly things you pass judgment on me for. While you're at it, tell the pastor with his hypocritical-sneaky-sinful-perverted ass that he could probably save more souls if he wasn't sitting at home lurking on Facebook!"

I hadn't meant to disclose any of that to my mother, but I let my anger get the best of me. I sat holding the phone both fuming and slightly saddened that my mother chose to defend Pastor McCaulley's behavior but only had negative things to say to me, her one and only child. There was silence on the other end of the phone for what felt like forever but actually only a few seconds.

"Toi," she sighed. "Baby, I am so sorry to hear that you have made such a mess of your life…the devil has obviously won and now the only thing I can offer you is prayer."

"Thank you for that, mama," I said sarcastically. "I can always depend on you to make me feel worse than I did before speaking with you. And you wonder why daddy barely says two words to you."

"Now you listen here—"

She didn't get the chance to complete her thought. I hung up on her. I sat at my desk, infuriated with the events of the day. From Lisa to my mother. I toiled with posting a note on my Facebook page advising my family and friends that any lewd pictures or post attached to my name are not being made by me due to a hacked account; however, I decided not to. I was not in the mood to explain myself to anyone and if people wanted to know my side of the story they could contact me and if they didn't, they could kiss my ass!

*****

I sat on the sofa with my legs pulled up to my chest, and my laptop sitting on the coffee table in front of me. After my argument with my mother I decided to take the rest of the day off. It was a wise choice, considering my phone was blowing up with calls and messages from family and friends, asking me if I was aware someone had photoshopped a picture of me onto Facebook. I knew damn well the picture was legit but I rode with the photoshop lie. It sounded better than admitting to all of them what was currently going on in my life. The only two people I told the truth to, besides my mother, were my besties.

Later, the two of them came over with Seagram's strawberry daquiri mix and a load of questions.

"First of all, why am I just *now* finding out he's married?" Anitra questioned me.

She was aware that Carlton and I were still seeing each other but she was clueless to his marital status. LaShay, on the other hand, knew less than 12 hours after I found out. Between the two of them LaShay was the less judgmental. I already knew what I was doing, I didn't need my best friend playing judge.

"Because she didn't want to deal with your dramatics," LaShay answered for me.

"What?" Anitra asked, with her mouth wide open. She touched her hand to her cleavage while shaking her head. "What dramatics?"

"Those," LaShay and I said in unison.

She looked from one of us to the other while sipping from the glass in front of her. "No, you two just knew what I was going to say," she said swallowing hard. "You are dead-ass wrong, Toi, sleeping with a married man."

"You're entitled to your opinion," I told her. "However, you have no room to judge."

"She's right, Anitra," LaShay agreed. "Let she that hath not sinned toss the...well, y'all know the rest."

I looked at LaShay then shook my head. "He that is without sin, cast the first stone," I said, correcting her.

"I told you y'all knew the rest," LaShay said, twisting her lips. "Thank you for that, Miss Auto Correct." It was obvious that when I went back to church, I needed to bring along my friend.

"As a *wife,*" Anitra said, clearing her throat, "I know how it feels to have your marital bond threatened."

"Who threatened your marital bond?" LaShay asked sarcastically. "Don't nobody want Kelvin."

"Keep on," Anitra said, sucking her teeth. "I'm just saying, we've had our share of drama, and the last thing you need during those times is for another sister to be pushing up on your man. We as women need to look out for each other."

"We as women need to take care of home," LaShay said.

"Spoken by a *single* woman," Anitra said, rolling her eyes.

"I'd rather be happily *single* then *married* and miserable," LaShay told her.

I looked at Anitra, awaiting her comeback. When she didn't reply I decided to jump in and try to calm the obvious tension.

"Listen, I know how I went about things was wrong," I admitted. "I can't change that nor can I change the fact that I want him to be a part of my life."

"Why so soon?" Anitra questioned. "You barely know him."

"Feelings don't require a lot of time Anitra," LaShay advised her.

"Maybe not but there seems to be a pattern," Anitra said, looking at me.

"What pattern?" I asked, confused.

"You did this with Justin," Anitra reminded me. "Met him one day and you were caught up the next."

"So?" I questioned, slightly offended.

"So look how that ended," she said sarcastically.

"Carlton isn't Justin," LaShay piped in. "And she doesn't need you reminding her of a damn thing...she lived it." It was obvious that LaShay was just as tired as I was of hearing Anitra's lecture.

Anitra's expression softened slightly. "You're right. I was wrong for that. Listen Toi, I just want the best for you." She paused, then looked at LaShay. "For both of you. And if you're happy then so be it...but how do we know if he did it to her that he won't do it to you?"

"I don't know," I said honestly. "But that's the chance I chose to take and I'm willing to deal with whatever consequences arrive."

"I just hope he's worth it," Anitra sighed. "And pray that he's who he claims to be."

"Me too," I agreed.

"So what are we going to do about wifey?" LaShay asked, changing the subject. "All those in favor of beating her ass for the little stunt she pulled, raise your hand." She shot her hand in the air then looked at me. Anitra followed suit and put her hand in the air too.

"Really? You too, Anitra?" I asked, laughing lightly.

"You may have been wrong but she's lucky she still has all her teeth and her hair," she said. "Beat down! Clearly that's what's she asking for."

"Maybe," I sighed. "But what will it solve? It won't change the fact that she's already put me and my business out there. I think it's better if I just let this whole thing die down."

"Well if it doesn't," LaShay said, smacking her lips. "I'll personally beat that ass."

*****

I was in the middle of searching the Internet to see if there were any other posts about me when Carlton knocked on the door.

"Hey beautiful," he smiled.

"Hey," I sighed.

"What's wrong?" he asked, stepping inside.

"Lisa," I said, walking back over to the sofa then plopping down.

"What about her?"

He walked over and sat beside me. I blew lightly through my parted lips, then turned the laptop so he could see the screen. He stared at the screen then frowned.

"Is that…"

"The picture from your phone," I answered, watching him. "Lisa posted it on Facebook this morning…actually, she hacked me, then posted under my account. Oh, and this is after she called me this morning." I explained to him everything that had taken place that day, right down to my conversation with my mother. "You need to check her, Carlton. I'm at my breaking point."

Carlton ran his hands across his face while shaking his head. "Baby, I'm so sorry, she probably got the picture the night she called you from my phone," he said. He closed the laptop then pulled me into his arms. "She shouldn't have done that. I'll speak to her."

"Thanks," I said. "Hopefully, now that she's humiliated me courtesy of the World Wide Web, she'll be content. Besides, in a couple of days this will die down and everyone will be on to the next scandal or half-naked female." I stroked his cheek with my fingertips gently before giving him a quick kiss on the mouth.

*****

Rubbing my eyes I stared in the darkness. Carlton lay on his back with his arm wrapped around my waist. I slowly eased his arm from around me, not wanting to disturb him as I slid out of bed. He turned slightly then continued to sleep peacefully. I cut my eyes at the alarm clock sitting on the nightstand, it was 3:00 am yet my landline was ringing off the hook. I eased out the bedroom and hurried across the carpeted floor to the end table where I had the phone charging. There were only two people who used my home number, my mother and people who dialed the wrong number.

"Hello," I asked, yawning lightly.

"Hey girl! It's Lisa. Did I wake you?"

"Lisa?" I asked, groggy and surprised. I was now wide awake. "Why are you calling me? And how did you get this number?!" I knew for a fact that she hadn't gotten it from Carlton's phone. Hell, he didn't get it until after he left her!

"I have my ways," she chanted. "In fact, I'm very resourceful... Toi LeAnna Underwood." *No, she didn't just use my entire government name!* "Store manager at Fashionista. Virgo..."

Maybe it was because I was still slightly sleepy but there sounded like there was something different about her tone. *Maybe it's the crazy*, I thought.

"Somewhere in those resources of yours do you think you can find a little something I like to call leave me the fuck alone?" I was cursing out of shear frustration and the fact that this heifer was on the phone sounding happy go lucky like the two of us didn't have issues!

"Ha ha ha," she cackled. "Good one. But look, girl, I'm looking for Carlton is he there?"

"Excuse me?"

"Carlton, is he there?" She asked again. "I was trying to see if he wanted to have breakfast with CJ later this morning. Spend some father son time together."

"First of all it's 2 in the morning," I said, through clenched teeth. "Second, Carlton has a phone...why didn't you call him?"

"Because," she said, flatly, "One of the quickest ways to reach a pimp is through his hoes."

She had officially pushed my last button.

"I got your hoe," I said, loudly.

"No, you *are* the hoe," she stated. "And I could actually respect you if that was all that you were, but you're a hoe and a liar. You need to commit to just one, those are serious professions to maintain and both are fulltime."

"Are you on something?" I asked, frowning. "Seriously. Or are you just crazy as hell?"

"Neither," she said. "I'm scorned and we both know what that means."

I wasn't shaken in the least bit by the tone of her voice or the obvious threat she was dropping. "I'm going to ask you one more time," I said. "Leave me alone."

"Mmph," she grunted. "Or what?"

"You heard what I said," I told her. "Conversation over."

I returned to my bed still fuming from my phone call with Lisa and tired as hell, mentally and physically. I don't know how long I had been sleeping but my rest was disrupted once again. This time it was the sound of Carlton's car alarm wailing.

"Carlton, wake up," I said, shaking him lightly.

"What is it, babe?"

"Your alarm." I yawned.

I moved from my position on his chest so that he could get up, then curled back up with his pillow. I was alerted of his return by the sound of the front door slamming and him blasting out obscenities.

"Fucking bitch!" he ranted.

I quickly tossed the covers back and hurried into the living room. I had never seen or heard him so upset. He paced back and forth across the living room floor wearing nothing but a T-shirt and boxers, running his hands across his head. His biceps appeared to bulge from underneath his shirt.

"What's wrong?" I asked.

"Look outside," he barked, pointing to the door.

I contemplated going back to the bedroom to get my shoes but my curiosity got the best of me. I opened the door, then crossed through the breezeway to the parking lot wearing nothing but a thin T-shirt and short shorts. The night air caused my nipples to harden and poke through my shirt as I stared at Carlton's car in utter and complete shock. His paint job looked like a two-year old had attempted to write their name in it. There were marks and indentations from the hood to the door where someone had keyed it.

"Damn," I whispered, shaking my head as I surveyed the damage. I shot a quick glance at my own vehicle, which was parked next to Carlton's. Everything looked intact but I decided to do a quick walk around just to be sure. After I saw everything was on the up and up I went inside. I stepped inside and caught Carlton on the phone arguing with someone.

"I know it was you!" He yelled. "You're following me now?

What the fuck ever."

I eased down in the chair watching him go back and forth with whom I assumed was Lisa on the phone.

"Bitch, wait till I get there," he threatened. He dropped his phone in his pocket then snatched his keys up off the coffee table.

"Carlton, I don't think you should go over there," I said, standing. "Especially when you're so angry."

"I'm fine," he said. He stomped out the room only to return a few minutes later, fully dressed in sweats and sneakers. "I'll be back."

"But baby," I said, following him to the door. "That's what she wants. She wants you to go over there and do something that will land you in jail. You have to outsmart her at her own game. Call the police, get it on record, but don't go over there, not when you're angry."

He looked at me then exhaled. "What would I do without you?" he asked, shaking his head.

"Probably five to ten," I teased, trying to lighten his mood. He laughed slightly but it was obvious he was still thinking of going through with his original plan, which I was sure would lead to him kicking Lisa's boney ass.

"I'll call James so we can file another report," I said.

"Don't worry about it," he said "I'll handle this with her personally. Not tonight but tomorrow."

"Are you sure?"

"Positive," he said. "Okay."

He pulled me to him then kissed me softly on my forehead. "I love you," he whispered.

I pulled back and smiled. "Do you really?"

"Yes."

"Good," I said. "I love you too."

# Chapter 26

## Lisa

"I can't believe you blasted her on Facebook," I laughed as Gabe and I sat in his den. He invited me over after work to look at some new handbags he had recently acquired. Once I got there he explained he was the one that hacked Toi's account and basically made her one of many Facebook tramps for that day. I'll admit it was wrong, but it also made me feel kind of warm and fuzzy inside. I knew Gabe's actions weren't completely unselfish; he had his own personal reasons for disliking Toi. He explained that he first met her at the store where she works and she threatened to have him arrested.

"I can't stand a woman who looks down on another human being."

From the way he described her, Toi was stuck up and had a stank attitude. Under different circumstances I wouldn't have judged her based off another person's opinion, but she *was* sleeping with my husband.

"Why do you think she's so determined to continue to see Carlton?" he asked. "She's one of those sisters who thinks she's entitled to any and all black men."

"Did she say that?"

"Not directly but look at how she's handling the situation. I mean any normal woman would have run in the opposite direction by now. Yet she stays..."

"Maybe she really cares about him," I suggested. "Or maybe he keeps begging her back." I hated to admit the latter of the two, but I knew it was a great possibility.

"Nonsense," Gabe said flatly. "Carlton has no reason to beg. Look at what he's got waiting." He nodded his head in my direction.

"True," I said. "But we never know what's being said."

"I still disagree."

"So, how did you get that picture?" I inquired, changing the subject.

I knew Carlton didn't give it to him. Carlton was a cheater but he was still a gentleman. He would never share something that was meant for his eyes only.

"Carlton had it in his phone," he said. "I did a little investigating when he came by to watch the game one night. Sometimes all the answers we need can be located in that little device."

"Wow," I said.

"I think this move will help Toi see that Carlton is not what she needs," he said. "And she should cut all ties expeditiously."

"We'll see," I said. I looked at my watch and saw that time had passed effortlessly since I arrived. "I better get going, I have got to pick up CJ from my aunt's."

"Before you do," Gabe said, raising his finger. "I got a hot little number that I think you would look superb on you."

"I don't know," I said. "I really should be going."

"It'll only take a minute," he said. "And if you like it you can consider it a gift."

I'm always down for a freebie. "Okay," I agreed.

"I let you try it on in the master bath," He said. "I have a three-way mirror inside."

It was the first time I had ever seen Gabe's bedroom and bath but both were tastefully decorated in gold and black. His had a platform bed with a huge wooden headboard that went midway up the wall. In the center of the board there was a large G embossed in the wood. The bed was covered with a black velvet comforter that had elegant gold trim. Gabe's bathroom looked more like a mini spa. There was a separate shower and double vanities with black marble counter tops, and a black garden tub. Along the eggshell walls sat iron candlestick holders with gold pillar candles gracing the plate of each one. The room and bathroom were clearly decorated with a man's touch, but a woman could easily appreciate and feel comfortable in.

The dress Gabe gave me was a cherry, one-shoulder, draped evening dress and it looked fabulous on me. I stood admiring myself in the floor-length mirror inside Gabe's bathroom telling myself that when Carlton and I got back on track, I would make sure he took me somewhere to flaunt the dress.

I slipped the dress off over my head, then returned it to its hanger. I stood wearing nothing but my panties, studying the details of my body in the mirror. I couldn't help but to compare myself to what I imagined Toi looked like without her clothes. She was bigger than me but she wasn't fat, just curvy. Was that the reason Carlton seemed so obsessed with her? I heard a noise coming from the bedroom. I covered my breasts with my arms then peeked out. The bedroom was empty but the door was slightly ajar. I thought I closed it on my way in? I dismissed the notion then quickly put on my clothes; I had to go get my son.

G STREET CHRONICLES

A NEW URBAN DYNASTY

WWW.GSTREETCHRONICLES.COM

# CHAPTER 27

## Toi

The store looked immaculate and I was extremely proud of how hard my staff had worked to help get things in order. I was completely confident my boss, Dallas, would give us an A+ later when she arrived for her visit. In the meantime I was blushing like a schoolgirl from Carlton's surprise visit to the store. He arrived carrying a long gold box containing two dozen long-stemmed red roses. After his visit with his attorney, he was all smiles and for me the smile was contagious. I thought I would never see him smile again after Lisa vandalized his car but after a couple days and a fresh new paint job he was back to his old self.

"Baby, that was so sweet," I gushed. The two of us stood inside the store by the registers.

"You're so sweet," he said. "Despite everything you've remained a sweetheart and patient and I just want you to know that I appreciate you."

"I appreciate you too," I said, sincerely.

Carlton was like my prince charming. Whenever the two of us had overnight visits, which was often, he cooked, cleaned, and treated me like a queen. It was easy to see why Lisa was having such a hard time letting go. I was at that place with my feelings where I wanted to tell the world I loved him and I wanted to be with him every second I could. My feelings had me second-guessing the decision we made not to live together. However, I knew that having his own place for CJ to visit was mandatory, considering the fact that Lisa would soon receive divorce papers along with Carlton's request for joint custody. I was confident that after our last conversation, Lisa had gotten the message because I had yet to receive another phone call or had any other problems out of her. When it came down to Carlton, Lisa continued to demand that he see their son on her terms, although he was still paying the bills at their home and she still had access to his bank account. I was not nor did I have any intentions to trip about the financial situation because I had my own and money was not the reason that I wanted to be with him.

"I better get going," he said. "I'm going grocery shopping later so think about what you want for dinner and text me."

"Get whatever you want," I said sweetly. "I'm cooking tonight."

"What about dessert?"

"Whatever you like," I said.

"I'll take a nice piece of you." He smiled suggestively.

"You can have it all," I whispered, before giving him a peck on the lips.

I didn't want to show too much affection due to my employees being present and their being nosey, so I kept it PG.

"Sounds like a plan," he said.

*****

"Toi, the store looks great," Dallas commented, as the two of us walked along the sales floor.

"Thank you," I said, smiling brightly. "I have a wonderful staff and everyone contributes."

"I had originally planned to visit last week," she explained. "But due to some issues with one of my other stores I had to postpone." She shook her head, causing her red curls to sway back and forth. "I am so glad you are not among my 'problem' children. There is always drama with some of my other managers."

"I completely understand," I said, reassuringly. "And I don't have time for drama."

Lisa popped in my head. "Yep, drama free," I said.

"Well, good and again, I say you are doing a great job." She smiled, then patted me on the shoulder. "Keep up the good work and one day you may be doing my job."

"I'm shooting for it," I said, confidently.

The two of us continued to talk and go over minor details about plans for the upcoming in-store promotions. After giving me one more 'atta girl', Dallas departed to visit our sister store. For lunch I decided to treat my team to Chloe's favorite; chicken. I walked out the door with my head held high, swaying on my heels while still basking in the joy of getting a good review from my DM. I was midway to my car when I heard a woman calling my name.

"Hey, Toi!"

I looked to my left and saw Nesha walking in my direction. I hadn't seen her since the day we met but she looked fabulous. She wore a cute white eyelet dress that stopped just above her knees with hot pink pumps. The micro-braids were gone and she was now wearing her hair in a straight, auburn-tinted style that fell just below her shoulders.

"Hey Nesha," I smiled.

She walked up and gave me a friendly hug before stepping

back to look at me.

"You are glowing," she commented. "You look good."

I had to admit, I felt good too. That morning I had chosen to wear a red chiffon cap-sleeve top and leopard-print pencil skirt for the day. I slipped on a pair of red, five-inch heels, pulled my hair to the side, and looked and felt like money.

"Look at you," I said. "Big change from the micros."

She touched her hand to her hair. "My baby wanted me to change it up sexy but classy," she said. "This wig is so damn hot but he loves it. She rolled her eyes while shaking her head. "The things we do for love," she said.

"Tell me about it," I laughed. "Well, you're rocking it."

"Thanks, girl," she said, politely. "I bought it from Gabe."

"He's a jack of all trades. Huh?" I said, with slight sarcasm.

I had chosen not to tell Carlton about his hitting on me but I still couldn't get over how dirty he was.

"Yes ma'am," Nesha said, enthusiastically. "He has weaves, wigs, shoes, dresses, bags, watches. . .whatever you need. Shopping at his spot is like going to the mall. Seriously. Electronics. . .you name it he's got it."

"Umm," I said. I knew she was also close to Gabe and I didn't want to say anything to offend her so I kept my opinions on Gabe to myself.

"You're leaving?" Nesha asked, changing the subject.,

"Just to go get lunch," I said. "What are you up to?"

"Nothing but a little bit of shopping. Gabe didn't have anything that interested me and I wanted your help picking out a couple of pieces."

"Why don't you ride with me," I suggested. "I'm just running over to Popeyes then we can come back and get our shop on."

She flashed her brown eyes at me. "Cool," she said.

I kept my eyes on the road while listening to Nesha describe her dating experiences before she met Quinton. She shared with me the tale of a man she was dating whom she thought she would someday marry, until she paid him a surprise visit one day only to find he was in bed with another woman.

"Girl, I tried my best to break out every window in that apartment," she chuckled. "And would have if I had found a rock big enough."

"A mess." I laughed.

"I know. Straight crazy in love." We both laughed.

"I've been there before," I confessed.

"What? When?"

"Two years ago," I stated. I opened up and shared the story of Justin and Peaches, I even told her about the night he dumped me.

"I know looks are deceiving," she said, looking over at me. "But you do not look like a killer."

"I'm not," I agreed. "How do you think I ended up smashing into a car?"

We both laughed again. It's amazing how what had been so heartbreaking before could now bring comical relief.

"Have you told Carlton?" She asked.

"Um…no," I said with raised eyebrows. "I didn't want to scare him off."

"Trust me Toi, he is used to crazy. Look at who he married."

"True," I agreed.

"Although Lisa is crazy in rare form," she stated.

"Don't I know it," I said, thinking about all the drama she'd brought me.

"I see why Carlton wants to break free." She paused. "And I don't blame you for not telling him about your past run in with your ex," Nesha said, quickly changing the subject. "After all, I'm sure you don't know all the women from his past."

"You have a point," I said. "And I don't want to. Some things are better left unknown."

She nodded her head in agreement. "I guess you're right," she said.

Her mood appeared to change and so did the vibe inside my vehicle. I suddenly felt that there was more she wanted to say but chose not to share.

"How long have the two of you known each other?" I asked, curious.

"For about seven years now."

"You met through Quinton?"

"Actually, no. Carlton introduced me to Quinton. I met Carlton at the gas station off Jordan Lane. I had a flat one night and he came up and offered to help. We started talking, exchanged numbers, and ended up being cool. We were practically inseparable at one time. That's how I met Gabe. They were roommates at the time."

"I never knew the two of them were roommates," I said honestly.

"Yep, for a short time," she said. "That was right after he and his ex-wife Carolyn went through their divorce."

"So Gabe was once married?" I was taking in all of the gossip Nesha was providing.

"Three times from what I've been told," she said.

"I see why he's single," I said. "He's probably tired."

"It wouldn't surprise me if there was a bride number four in his future." Nesha exhaled. "Gabe has a way with women. He knows how to get what he wants."

*He doesn't know that well,* I thought. I was thinking of his failed attempt to hit on me.

"He's definitely something," I said.

"Yep, complete opposite of Carlton," she said. "But I guess opposites attract even when it comes to friendship."

"So you and Carlton use to be really tight," I said lightly.

"Yes, but it was never like that," she said, quickly. "Not like a couple. Just really good friends."

It was obvious she was reading my mind because that was going to be my next question, had they ever dated?

"Carlton has always looked at me like a sister," she said. "He's always looked out for me. He's a good guy, real good. He deserves the best."

There was a certain hint of admiration in her voice that made me question her feelings for Carlton. She stated he looked at her like she was a sister, but she never said she looked at him in the same way.

"Oh, thank you," I said. "For helping Carlton get the room."

I had almost forgotten that Nesha had assisted Carlton with surprising me with the room at the hotel the night Lisa showed up.

"You're welcome," she said, smiling sweetly. "I'm always happy to help. I loved how Carlton had everything set up for you."

"Wasn't it nice?" I smiled, appreciatively.

"Yes, enough to make a woman jealous."

There was suddenly a strong undercurrent in her tone. Something that told me my thoughts were true. She wanted Carlton.

"I mean make some women jealous," she said laughing lightly.

It was too late for her to attempt to play it off. Her feelings were obvious.

# Chapter 28

## Lisa

I sat behind the large glass receptionist booth playing solitaire on the PC while waiting for Ellen's next client. I was bored almost to the point where at any moment I could just bolt out the front door, but I told myself to tough it out; I only had two hours to go. Since Carlton had yet to return home I took on a full-time position as the receptionist at my Aunt Ellen's salon so I could have additional spending money to take care of my personal needs. In his absence the extra little things he once footed the bill for, such as my hair and shopping, fell to me and my pockets. Aunt Ellen reminded me that I was once independent before I met him and this was my time to show him I could do it without him. I heard every word she was saying, but screw that. I'm the wife and it wasn't fair for me to have the title but some other broad was receiving the cash flow. Yes, the bills were still being paid but I didn't give a damn. I earned my keep when I said 'I do' and birthed Carlton a son. However, I knew our time apart was essential to his rediscovering who he once was.

My decision to control how and when he visited was simply my way of reminding Toi who held the power in our situation. I couldn't understand why she didn't get it. No matter how

Carlton and I argued or he left, we had a child together and our bond was unbreakable. The two of us always came back to one another even if it was only for CJ. It was only a matter of time before he got tired of his supervised visitation, came to his senses and returned home. In the meantime I planned to make things as uncomfortable as possible for the two of them. Every time Carlton didn't get a chance to spend time with his son, I wanted him to remember why when he looked at Toi. Why should she get the right to screw with my marriage then just live like everything is fine? She shouldn't. I hadn't received any other packages or surprises and I couldn't help but conclude it was because Toi now had what she wanted; Carlton. However, I was hoping she wasn't getting too comfortable. It was only a matter of time before their little affair was finally over, once and for all.

The door chimed as a tall blonde entered the salon. The woman was provocatively dressed in a short, printed, knit mini-dress that hugged every inch of her curves.

"How may I help you?" I asked.

"Do you guys wax eyebrows?"

"Yes, we do."

"How much?"

"$15.00"

"Cool," she smiled. She had a bubbly personality but there was something about her voice that gave me the impression she was dumb as a rock.

"Wait! Are you Lisa Thomas?" She asked, batting her brown eyes at me.

"Yes."

"Cool!" she cheered. She reached inside her handbag then pulled out papers. "Lisa, you've been served," she said, extending the papers out to me. Her voice and everything about her demeanor changed. Maybe she's not as dumb as I thought. She looked at me with raised eyebrows while waiting for me to take the papers from her hand. I snatched them so hard I almost tore the ends. She laughed.

"Have a nice day," she said, before spinning on her heels and marching out the door.

*That bitch is filing a complaint against me*, I thought, assuming the papers were in regards to Toi. I opened the pages and was greeted with the words: **Petition for Dissolution of Marriage**.

For a brief moment I thought I was seeing things. I closed my eyes then slowly opened them, focusing on the papers again. I had it right the first time, the papers were my notification that Carlton had filed for divorce. This was not what I was expecting.

"Aunt Ellen, I have an emergency," I yelled across the salon.

I grabbed my bag and phone then marched out the door before she had the opportunity to question me. Six years, I recited to myself. Six damn years and this is how he does it? For six years I had been Carlton's everything and this is how he repays me? I climbed into my car then slammed the door. In less than sixty seconds I had the engine roaring and I was zooming out the parking lot. I pulled my phone out of the middle console and hit speed dial 2.

"Hello," Carlton answered.

"You son of a bitch," I yelled. "You filed for divorce?"

"Yes, I've had time to think and I'm done," he said calmly.

"What?" I screamed. "Done? Carlton, are you serious?"

"Lisa, we've been wrong for a very long time. And it's obvious we've both moved on."

I was clueless as to what he meant. He may have moved on but I was still very much in love with him.

"What are you talking about, Carlton?" I asked. "I'm still here waiting for us to make things right."

"Good one," he laughed. "The evidence would prove otherwise."

"What evidence?" I questioned, confused. "I've done everything to prove myself to you!"

"And I've done nothing?" He asked. "I stayed longer than I should have."

I knew his question was a rhetorical one, I chose not to answer.

"That's what I thought," he said. "Listen, I think it's best if we make this as easy and quick as possible. Sign the papers, Lisa. You can keep the house and the car. All I want is the freedom to see my son when and how I like."

"You think I'm going to allow you to flaunt that wench in front of my child?" I asked. "No way, Carlton!" *He had chosen her but I'd be damned if she played Mommy to my child!*

"Then I'll ask for sole custody," he said. "And I'll dictate how and if you see *my* son."

"I am his mother! No one is going to keep him from me."

"Then do the right thing, Lisa."

"Go to hell!" I said before hanging up.

I dropped the phone back in the console then merged onto the on-ramp, headed toward Fashionista. If Carlton didn't want to hear me, I was going to make damn sure his little girlfriend did!

# Chapter 29

## Toi

"That is super hot," I said, admiring Nesha.

She stood in front of me with her hands on her hips modeling one of the newest pieces I'd received earlier in the week. The dress was black and white retro, above the knee with a fitted bodice.

"It is definitely outside of my box," she laughed, looking at herself in the floor-length mirror.

"I like it on you," I said. "It's sexy but classy. Now all you need is some shoes. What size do you where?"

She hesitated then sighed, "I wear a twelve," she said. *Damn*, I thought.

I looked at her feet. *How had I missed them?* "Oh," I said, trying to play off my shock. "We only carry up to a ten."

"Toi!"

I turned at the sound of my name being called only to see Lisa standing in front of the entrance. Her face was flushed and I knew that her presence meant drama.

"What is she doing here," I said aloud.

"Toi!" She called again.

There were several other customers present in the store, and

Lisa had captured their attention as well as mine.

"I'm not in the mood for this bullshit," I said, as I started to walk off. How dare she show up at my place of business?

"Wait Toi," Nesha said, grabbing my arm. "Let me go talk to her."

"Naw, I got it," I said, heated.

"Toi, this is your job," Nesha reasoned. "You don't need this. Not here in front of your employees and customers. She's probably pissed because of the papers."

I had forgotten that Carlton said Lisa was going to be served with divorce papers. Clearly Lisa had come to blame me for it.

"I'll be back," Nesha said quickly. "Just stay here."

She hurried off before I could protest again. There was something in my gut advising me that I should try to talk to Lisa myself but I held back, I watched as Nesha walked up to her, then wrapped her arm around Lisa's shoulder and led her outside. I moved in between the clothes racks and watched the two of them. From where I stood, if I didn't know otherwise, I would say they were the best of friends. I watched as Lisa stood with her face covered, obviously to prevent others from seeing her tears, while Nesha stood with her arms wrapped around her, consoling her closely. It was obvious there was more to their friendship than Nesha had told me.

*****

Carlton leased a nice two-bedroom, two-bath townhouse on the northwest side of the city. The unit had recently been remolded and updated with stainless steel appliances and granite countertops. It also came completely furnished, and had a small area adjacent to the patio that was completely fenced in that had just enough room for CJ to play whenever he visited in the future. It was perfect for Carlton and CJ and even I loved it.

"That smells good," he whispered kissing my earlobe.

For dinner he requested stuffed pork chops, potatoes, and green beans. I was thankful he had chosen something that was both quick and easy. I was slightly exhausted from the days' events.

"Thank you," I said. "Another ten minutes and I'll fix your plate."

"Sounds good," he said, rubbing up against my backside.

"Don't start," I warned.

"I won't," he laughed. "I'll wait until dessert."

"Nesha came by the store today."

"Really?" he asked.

"Yes, I helped her pick out a few things."

"That was nice of you"

"Yeah, we talked for awhile," "I said. "She told me how you two met and how you introduced her to Gabe and Quinton."

"That seems like forever," he said. He stepped back, leaned against the counter and looked at me. "It's funny how time flies."

"How long has she been close to Lisa?"

"She's not. I mean they tried to be friends when Lisa and I first got together, but they drifted apart," he said, frowning. "Why?"

"Lisa stopped by to see me," I said.

"When?"

"Today at work," I said, "I didn't speak with her. Nesha was still there and she volunteered to see what she wanted."

"What happened after that?"

"After crying on Nesha's shoulder. She left without speaking to me," I said, "When I asked Nesha about the conversation she stated that Lisa just wanted to vent."

"I guess it's a good thing Nesha was there," he said nonchalantly.

"I don't know," I said. "The two of them looked awfully chummy. What if Nesha had something to do with Lisa coming to the hotel?"

"I don't think she would do that," he said. "I mean why, would she?"

"Because she wants you," I said

"No," he said, laughing "Nesha's always been like a sister to me."

"I know," I said. "But that doesn't change how she looks at you or what she *wants* to be."

He looked like he was actually considering what I was saying. "No, I still don't think she would do something like that." He kissed my cheek before walking off. I shook my head. *Sometimes men were so damn gullible.*

# Chapter 30

## Lisa

Nesha's voice had been the calm in the storm. She reminded me that the last thing I wanted was for Toi to have yet another thing to run back and tell Carlton about me. She even suggested that I may want to consider giving Carlton what he wanted. I heard every word Nesha said about knowing how to let go but I was not giving up on my marriage. If Carlton wanted a divorce he was going to have to hold me down and force me to sign otherwise ride it out by default. I refused to sign willingly. My phone rang for the tenth straight time that morning. I knew even before I looked at the screen that it was Carlton. I had originally agreed to let him see CJ but since I received his little surprise paperwork, I changed my mind. I pushed CJ in the grocery buggy while rolling down aisle 15 of Publix Supermarket toward the checkout. I was so focused on beating the next person to the line that I didn't even notice Sasha.

"Lisa!" She smiled, brightly.

"Uh...Hey!" I gave her the quick once-over with my eyes. I instantly felt insecure with my ponytail and sweats. My friend looked great in her fitted jeans and one-shoulder blouse. Her hair was cut in a short,layered style with soft cinnamon highlights.

"This is sad," she said, extending her arms to me.

I reluctantly stepped inside her embrace then quickly pulled away.

"What is?"

"Us bumping into each other here ," she said. "We should have been gotten together by now."

"I know," I said.

"Hey cutie!" she said, pinching CJ's cheeks.

He smiled then winked. It was obvious he was going to be a charmer like his daddy.

"I've just been busy," I said.

"Trust me, I understand," Sasha said, flashing her brown eyes at me. "So how have you been?"

"I'm good and you?"

I was not in the mood for conversation, but it was obvious I was not going to be able to avoid. I moved up in the line while Sasha maneuvered her buggy in line behind me.

"I'm well," she said.

"Good," I said, loading my items on the belt.

I didn't ask about her husband because I did not want her asking about mine.

"I saw Carlton," she said, lowly.

*There goes wishful thinking,* I thought.

"Oh yeah. When?"

"The other night at the movies," she informed me, "with another woman."

The image of Carlton and Toi on their little date made me want to gun both of them down.

"Oh."

"He told me that the two of you are going through a divorce," she continued.

I loaded the last of my groceries on the belt then looked at her. "This is just a minor glitch," I said lightly "The two of us will have it worked out in no time."

Sasha frowned then sighed. "Lisa, you and I are better than that," she said, gently. "You don't have to lie."

"I'm not," I said.

"You are aware that he's with someone else?" She asked. "I met her. I mean he introduced her to me."

"I've met her too," I said nonchalantly. "No biggie. We'll work this out soon."

I could feel the flush falling over my face. I felt like I was standing under the heat of a spotlight as Sasha stared at me. How could Carlton? He knew Sasha was my friend. Why did he have to introduce Toi to her? Why couldn't he have made a feasible excuse. Hell, tell her she was his cousin, anything but the truth.

"$172.00, please," the young cashier said to me.

I quickly removed my debit card from my wallet then swiped it through the machine. I punched in my pin then hit enter to confirm my total.

"Minor setback," I smiled looking at Sasha.

"If you say so," she said, "but he sounded confident and sure of what he wanted."

I chose not to respond.

"Ma'am your card was declined," the cashier advised me.

"Let me try it again," I said. "I probably entered the wrong pin." I punched the numbers so quickly, I was sure I made an error. I waited for her to hand me my receipt.

"I'm sorry but it declined again," the cashier said.

"Run it as credit," I instructed.

I didn't know what was wrong with the damn card, but I needed to get out of line and away from Sasha as soon as possible.

"I'm sorry ma'am, would you like to use another form of payment?" the cashier asked.

I didn't have another form of payment and I didn't need one; I knew the account had more than enough to cover the bill. "I need to call BB&T," I said, referring to my bank. "Can you just leave this here until I get back?"

The chunky girl who couldn't have been older than seventeen looked displeased by my request and quite frankly she looked slightly annoyed. I was already embarrassed from the situation; the last thing she wanted was to add anger to the mix, with the mood I was in I was likely to slap her ass.

"Lisa," Sasha said softly, "I'll get it for you."

"What? Girl no, I just need to step outside and call to see what's going on," I said, shaking my head.

"Well, I can pay then once they work it out you can just pay me back," she insisted.

I heard a few grumbles from the other shoppers in line behind Sasha. I shot a look in their directions, ready to give them a piece of my mind.

"Please, Lisa," Sasha begged.

Ten minutes later I stood by the trunk of my car with a representative from the bank on the phone and Sasha standing beside me. I had already loaded the groceries in the trunk and CJ inside in his seat.

"Ma'am, this account has a zero balance," the representative advised me.

"What do you mean zero?"

"There was a funds transfer this morning," he advised. "To another account."

"I didn't authorize that!" I snapped.

"It was done online via online banking."

I immediately knew Carlton was responsible.

"Can you tell me where the money was transferred to?" I asked, biting my lip.

"To another checking account," he said.

"In whose name?"

"I can't disclose that," he said. "You're not authorized on that account."

"Thanks," I said sarcastically. I pressed the end button on my phone then stared at Sasha. I was humiliated.

"Don't worry about it," she said, before I had a chance to say anything. "Pay me back when you can." Her eyes were overflowing with pity.

"Thanks," I said, lowly.

"Lisa, I don't want to get in your business," she said soothingly. "But I think—"

"My marriage is not over," I said, cutting her off. "He will be back, Sasha. Please don't pass judgment on a five-minute conversation you had with Carlton. I know his heart and he loves me."

She sighed, then nodded her head. "Okay. Well, I gotta get my food home but call me, Lisa," she said. "If you need something or just to talk."

I nodded my head. "I'll get your money to you next week," I said.

"No worries," she smiled again.

I waited until I was in the security of my car to reach out to Carlton.

"Hello."

"You closed the account?" I yelled.

"No I transferred the funds," he corrected me. "I couldn't

close the account without your signature. "So I did the next best thing."

"You arrogant ass!" I screamed. "I had no money to buy groceries! If it wasn't for Sasha being in line behind me I would have had to leave without food. Food for your son."

"If my son needs food he needs to be with me," he said coldly. "I can afford to feed him. And if you can't…"

"What kind of man does that?" I asked, on the verge of tears. "Leaves his wife broke to prove a point?"

"What kind of woman uses her child as a rope in a tug-of-war?" he questioned. "And last time I checked, I pay for the utilities and the roof over your head. That's the kind of man I am! All I want is to see my son but you want to play this little game, so these are the consequences. If my son is hungry I'll bring him whatever he wants, but you're on your own. And I advise you, if you don't stop refusing to let me see him as I see fit, the next thing you'll be looking for is candles and matches. After that four stakes and a tent. I'm done dealing with you and your bullshit. Lisa, this marriage is over. You need to accept that."

"Six years, Carlton," I pleaded. "I gave you six years and you up and throw it all away for a woman you've known less than nine months? Why?"

"Love doesn't have a timeline, Lisa," he said. "I'm sorry you're hurt but I'm not sorry that I fell in love." He ended the call on that note. I sat in the car, slumped over the steering wheel overcome with emotion and engulfed in tears. This was not the man that I once knew, not the man I loved. It was obvious that man was gone. He hadn't said it before but this time he made it very clear. He was no longer in love with me but he was in love with her. I had no more fight left in me for this battle. They had won.

"Don't cry mommy," CJ called from the backseat.

I looked at my starry-eyed little boy and asked myself what lesson was I teaching him about women. What expectations was I setting for him about love. I couldn't stop the tears even if I wanted and I could no longer deny the truth. Thoughts of everything that had transpired between Carlton and me flooded my brain like the rising waters of a river and much like a dam when it's sustained more pressure than for which it is made; something inside of me snapped. I pressed the call button on my phone twice.

"Hello," Carlton answered loudly.

"Meet me at the house in an hour," I said, voice quivering from my tears. "CJ will be ready to go when you get there."

"Lisa, don't play with me," he said.

"I'm not," I said. "Come get your son. The game is over. I'm done."

"I'll be there," he said.

On the drive home I thought about my mother and sisters. Monica's words echoed in my ear. She was right. She was honest and real enough to know when to let go. As a woman I had to know when to let go.

I pulled into the driveway then assisted CJ out the back. I held my son's hand as I marched up the driveway lost in my thoughts.

"Go get your backpack, baby," I instructed him. "Daddy's coming to get you."

"Yay! Daddy!" He chanted down the hallway.

I went back outside, retrieving the groceries and bringing them inside. This was something I would never get used to… the little things that Carlton did that I was now responsible for. I shook my head. I put all the items away, then headed to CJ's bedroom to help him pack.

"I think you're going to need a little more than Spider-Man and Batman," I laughed.

There was nothing in his bag but the two action figures and a pair of shorts. He looked at me, laughed, then continued playing with the newest truck his father had bought him. I packed him enough clothes for several days, then carried his bag in the kitchen with me. I pulled the documents I had stuffed inside the top kitchen drawer out and sat down at the table with my pen. I scanned over them like I hadn't already scanned over them a thousand times. I was getting a decent deal from Carlton. The house, my car, and full assistance for six months until I got on my feet. I was getting much more than a lot of other women I'd seen in similar situations. I signed on the line designated for my signature. I was officially done. I folded the papers back neatly then stuffed them down in CJ's bag.

*****

Carlton came exactly one hour after our phone call. As soon as he stepped through the door, CJ came running with his backpack swinging over his shoulder. I couldn't deny that Carlton looked extremely happy and he smiled a smile that I hadn't seen in a very long time.

"You ready to go man?" he asked, lifting CJ over his head.

"Yessss," CJ screamed and laughed.

"Let's go," Carlton said, easing him back down on his feet.

I followed the two of them outside to the car. When he opened the door I saw that he was alone. After settling CJ in the back seat he looked at me then opened the driver's side door.

"Here you go," he said, reaching in his pocket. He pulled out his wallet and removed a $100 bill.

"I'm good," I said, putting my hand up. "Just pick up some things for CJ."

He looked surprised. "Are you sure?" he asked.

"I'm positive," I said.

"Okay, well I'll have him home tomorrow night."

"If not he has enough clothes to last until Tuesday." I told him.

"In that little bag?" He asked.

"Yep, but of course you have to iron them," I winked. "You know I couldn't make it that easy for your ass." I laughed lightly. Carlton stared at me like he thought I had lost my mind.

"Are you okay?" He asked, undoubtedly surprised by my mood.

"I'm good now," I said. "Better than I've been in a very long time. In fact I'm going to be just fine."

"Good," he said.

There was a moment of peaceful silence between us. "Well, I better get going," he said.

"One more thing," I said, touching his arm.

"What's that?"

I reached out extending my arms to him. He hesitated, then pulled me into his embrace. There was strength in the hug he gave me but I now could recognize that there was no love. Don't get me wrong, I knew he loved me but it wasn't the love that lives and forever are built on. It was the kind of love that two people share who have run their course, when both parties finally agree that they have come to the end of their race.

"I will always love you for who you were to me and for giving me CJ," I whispered in his ear. I pulled away then softly pressed my lips to his.

"Take care," I said backing away from the car. "CJ be good,

baby."

"Okay mommy!" he called.

I turned then walked back to my home with a smile on my face.

# CHAPTER 31

## Toi

CJ was one of the most beautiful little boys I had ever seen, and by far one of the sweetest. His lightly tan skin, jet-black curly hair, and big brown eyes made my heart melt at first sight. I'll admit, I was slightly nervous about our meeting; after all, I had no clue what his mother might have said about me, but as it turned out the child instantly clinged to me. He gave me an abundance of hugs and kisses that made me fall in love instantly.

When Carlton first moved into his new place the two of us decorated the second bedroom in Spider-Man and Batman furnishings from wall to wall. I even had a seamstress sew CJ a rug and comforter with one side Spider-Man and the other Batman. When CJ finally got to see the room his eyes lit up like it was Christmas morning.

"I think he likes it." Carlton laughed.

"I would say he loves it," I corrected him. I laughed while watching CJ hugged the walls, literally. "So how was Lisa?"

"She was good," he said. "I think she finally gets it."

I was relieved to hear this. "I'm extremely glad," I said. "I'm tired of fighting with her."

"I think she is too," he said. "I'm going to go fire up the grill…" He kissed me on the top of my head. "Be right back."

"Okay," I smiled. I walked into the bedroom and sat down on the edge of the bed. "Do you like your room, CJ?" I asked.

"Yeah," he said, looking over at me. "I have Batman and Spider-Man."

"You do? Where, at home?"

"Yea, but I brought 'em wit me," he said, running over to the bed.

"Can I see?"

"Yea, you can play wit 'em if you want."

"That's sweet," I smiled. "Thank you, but only if you'll play with me."

"Okay," he said, unzipping his bag. He turned the bag upside down dumping everything out.

"What's this?" I asked, picking up a stack of papers.

"Don't know," CJ shrugged, picking up his toys. "Do you wanna be Batman or Spider-Man?" I looked at the papers silently.

"Okay you can be Batman," CJ answered for me.

"I tell you what," I said, looking at him. "Why don't I go get Daddy? He's a way better Batman than me."

"'K."

I stroked the top of his curls, then excused myself from the bedroom. I didn't know if Carlton knew about the papers and he just wanted me to find them or if he even knew they were there. Either way I was thrilled. I could see Carlton through the open blinds, standing on the patio with his cellphone at his ear. His body stance and the way he paced back and forth told me that the conversation he was having was intense. I eased open the sliding door then stepped out on the patio. I didn't want to interrupt what was obviously a very heated conversation.

"I told you before," he said, with his back to me. "Get your emotions in check. I'm done going back and forth with you. Get over it."

"Carlton," I said softly.

"I gotta go," he said roughly.

He ended the call then turned around to look at me. "Hey babe," he said.

"Who was that?" I questioned.

"Lisa," he said shaking his head. "She's on the phone trippin'."

"I thought she was coming around," I said, moving closer to him. I was confused as to why a woman who not only allowed her child to finally meet her husband's girlfriend but also had signed the petition for divorce would now be giving him trouble. It didn't make sense. Yes, I still thought Lisa was crazy, but I thought she had at least put a cap on her crazy.

"I did too," he exhaled loudly. "But I called and reminded her about the papers and she went off."

I clutched the papers I found in CJ's backpack tightly in my hand. "What did she say?" I asked, sensing that something wasn't right.

"That she's not signing and all this bullshit," he explained. "That if I want the divorce then I better get ready to fight it out. Nonsense." He licked his lips while rubbing his hands together. "I'm not worried," he advised. "I know she'll come around."

"She must have come around sooner than you planned," I said, staring him in the eyes.

"What do you mean?"

"Does Lisa dot her I's with a smiley face?" I probed.

"Yes. Why?" He asked. He looked completely thrown off about my knowledge of that piece of information. "Don't tell me she sent you something. Is she still harassing you?"

"Nope," I said, extending my arm to him.

"What's this?" He asked, removing the papers from my hand.

"Your divorce papers. Lisa signed them." I announced. "They were tucked in CJ's bag."

I watched Carlton's eyes as they shifted from left to right while he read over the documents, verifying what I had already told him.

"That is her signature?" I asked. "Right?"

"Uh, yeah," he said, "it is."

"Great. So who were you on the phone with again?" I questioned.

"I told you babe," he said, walking up to me. "Lisa. I guess she was just trying to get me riled up for nothing. I hope she grows up soon. I'm going to go check on CJ. I'll be right back." He kissed me on my forehead then left me standing alone consumed by my thoughts of doubt.

# Chapter 32

## Lisa

"In an instant we throw in the towel," Gabe stated, shaking his head. The two of us sat in his den discussing my decision to sign the divorce papers.

"It's been longer than an instant," I reminded him. "I can't keep letting this situation break me down to the point that my son sees me bitter and broken. I don't want that kind of life. Hell, I've already allowed him to see and hear enough. No more."

"I can understand your concern," he said. "I just hate that the cards couldn't fall the opposite direction."

"The cards fell in the direction that we chose to play them," I stated. "It is what it is. Who knows, maybe someday we'll get it back. You never know."

I had been ignoring my urge to pee for almost an hour. My body finally decided enough was enough. "May I use your restroom?" I asked, standing before he answered.

"Of course you can," he said. "You know where it is."

"I think I remember," I said, rising from the sectional.

As I strolled down the carpeted hall looking at the closed doors, I realized I didn't have a clue which one of them was actually the bathroom. I knew from memory that the door at the end of the hall was Gabe's bedroom and although I could easily use his master bathroom, I felt some kind of way about being in other people's bedrooms without their direct permission. I finally decided to take a guess at it and opened the smallest door I saw. I figure it was either the bathroom or a closet. I turned the knob, then felt along the wall for the light switch. To my delight it was a bathroom. After handling my business, I returned to the den only to discover Gabe was no longer sitting where I left him. I opened the back door assuming he had stepped out onto this deck. The deck was empty also. I walked from the den through the kitchen to the other side of the house where Gabe housed his game room and office. I could hear the voices of two women coming from the office. He's got company. I hesitated, thinking I should turn around and not disturb their conversation.

However, my curiosity got the best of me. As I approached I saw the door to his office was slightly open and I could see him sitting at his desk, reclining in the leather chair with his arms propped behind his head. On the desk in front of him there was a large flat screen monitor along with a phone and square box that looked a lot like a piece of equipment you would see in a recording studio, only smaller. The monitor was on, displaying a bar chart with different stats in red and green pulsing up and down on the screen. I saw that Gabe was alone and assumed he had his friends on speaker, that was until I heard him speaking aloud. The female's voice I heard was his! He was using a voice transformer. I listened closely to hear who he was speaking to with the device.

"I told you to stay away from my husband," Gabe said. "That was all I asked of you but no, you refused to heed my warning. Now I guess there is only one thing left to do."

"I told you to stop calling me!"

"Well, I guess we both failed," Gabe said. "Now one of us is going to pay the ultimate price."

Are you threatening me, Lisa?"

I finally recognized the voice of the woman he was speaking to, it was Toi.

"No, I'm making you a promise, bitch," he said, before I heard a click.

My thoughts began to run rampant as I hurried away from the door toward the kitchen.

# CHAPTER 33

## Toi

I was surprised at work by the sound of my first stalker's voice, Lisa. My day had been going perfectly until she called, sounding off. I was beginning to think that she was bipolar or actually had multiple personalities. Nonetheless, it was obvious that Carlton was telling the truth about her and her erratic behavior. During our phone call she did everything but come out and say that she was going to kill me. To make matters worse, HPD was useless to me at the moment.

"She'll have to do something first," James explained, "come around or something that constitutes a warrant being issued. Technically from what you're describing, she didn't make a direct threat."

"Hell, that was a hint!" I said, annoyed.

"That's not enough," James said. "I'm sorry."

I wasn't even trying to hear that bullshit. How many people heard 'I'm sorry' right before they turned up dead?

"I'll talk to her again, Carlton said. Carlton advised me that he would handle it when he stopped by to see CJ later that evening, but I had little faith that his confronting Lisa was going to do a bit of good. I decided I needed to take matters in my own hands.

"Where does she live?" LaShay asked, over the phone.

"I have no clue," I said. "Somewhere in Madison."

"Let me call you back," she said.

Fifteen minutes later she called back. "Madison Cove," she said, as soon as I answered. "The address is…"

I quickly jotted down the information she provided.

"How did you get the address?"

"Robert," she sighed.

"Robert? Carlton's cousin Robert?" I asked, surprised.

"Yep,"

"I didn't know you had contact with him"

"Stay focused," she said, lightly. "This is not about me or my business."

"Maybe not, but I want details."

"You know the guy I've been seeing?" she asked, sighing loudly.

"The one you met at work?"

"Yes, that's him," she confessed. "He came into the pharmacy one day and the two of us started talking. I gave him my number and we've been dating ever since."

"I can't believe you didn't tell me," I said. "And he hasn't told Carlton."

"I threatened his ass, that's why," she said loudly. "And I saw no point in telling you. The two of us are just having a good time. Nothing serious, just sex."

"Mmm hum," I said, in disbelief.

"You heard me!"

"And he gave you the address," I said. I was happy but surprised.

"Of course he did," she said. "He can't stand Lisa and he loves my ass. Literally."

"TMI." I frowned.

"I'll see you when I get off," she said, ignoring my comment.

# CHAPTER 34

## Lisa

I decided the best way for me to address what I overheard at Gabe's was to be honest and direct about everything that had taken place. I didn't like the fact that he was pretending to be me while threatening Toi. What if something really did happen to her? All roads and fingers would point back to me. I decided to clear the air with Carlton with the hopes that he would arrange for Toi and I to have a sit-down.

"So Gabe was the one who posted Toi's picture on Facebook?" Carlton asked, looking across the table at me.

"Yes, and he called her pretending to be me," I confessed. "I heard him on the phone with her. He was threatening her."

"So why are you telling me this now?"

"So you can talk to him," I said. "Tell him to cut it out."

"And I should believe you, why?" he asked seriously.

"Carlton, why would I lie?"

"So you won't look like the hoe that's screwing one of her husband's closest friends."

"What are you talking about?" I asked, confused. "First of all, you're my soon to be ex-husband. Secondly I would never touch one of your friends."

"You and Gabe," he said, folding his hands together on the table. "He told me that the two of you hooked up. Actually he sent me a picture of you half naked in his bedroom."

"What? I've never…"

Flashbacks of the evening I tried on the dress popped in my head. "I was trying on a dress," I explained. "That's why I was half naked in his bedroom."

"Since when did you start hanging out with my friends?"

"The day I caught you at the hotel with Toi, Nesha texted me," I confessed. "That's how I knew where you were. After that Gabe stopped by here and he offered to help me."

He stared at me for a second then nodded his head. "I'll go out there tonight," he said "I'll talk to him then."

"Thank you."

"I'm going to go tuck CJ in before I leave," he said. "If that's all right with you."

"Sure."

I sat at the kitchen table drumming my fingers lightly while asking myself if I had done the right thing by telling Carlton. The sound of Carlton's cell phone vibrating loudly on the table disrupted my chain of thought. I looked from the hall to the phone. It was none of my business who was calling him but what if it was Toi? I still wanted to talk to her. The vibration stopped, only to start again five seconds later. I finally picked up the phone to see who it was. I entered CJ's birthday to unlock the phone, then looked at the screen.

*256-555-9666: see you tonight. XOXO*

"What the hell?" I questioned, aloud.

I scrolled through the message thread, displaying the messages that were sent between Nesha and Carlton. Once I concluded I had seen enough, I quickly put the phone back on the table while trying desperately to control what I was now feeling inside.

*****

I was still trying to process my thoughts when there was a knock at my door.

"Toi," I said, frowning.

She stood at my door with an expression that told me that she had no plans for her visit to be a friendly one. The female standing beside her was my confirmation of this. She cut her eyes at me, then frowned.

"What's that shit you've been talking?" she asked bluntly. She clutched her leather handbag close to her body. I exhaled through my parted lips but chose to ignore her question. If she wanted to hurt me she would have already.

"Come in," I said, looking at Toi. "We need to talk."

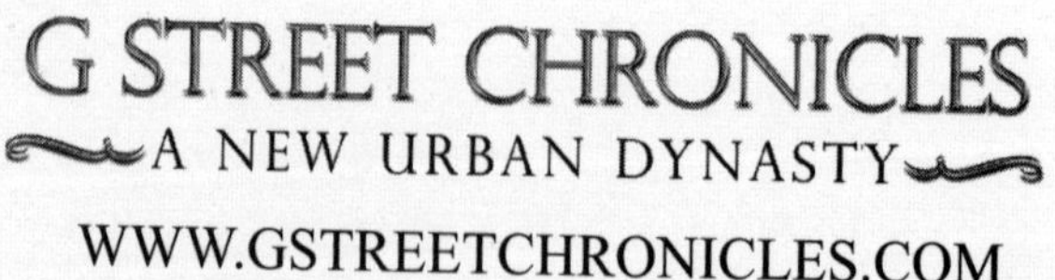
G STREET CHRONICLES
A NEW URBAN DYNASTY
WWW.GSTREETCHRONICLES.COM

# Chapter 35

## Toi

I stated that Lisa's voice sounded different sometimes when she called. I was right because it was Gabe and his twisted ass. I couldn't believe he was playing both sides in what I could only assume was his way of trying to help his friend Nesha cross out the competition. I wonder if Nesha was breaking him off too or was his motivation purely based on the fact that he already disliked me for our run-in at my store. A part of me wanted to believe Lisa was lying about Nesha's text message to Carlton but at that point, why would she lie? She signed the papers and she'd been cooperating with Carlton ever since. Plus, I knew in my heart that something wasn't right between Nesha and Carlton. My heart wanted it to be some other explanation or some valid reason but the only answer I came back to was the two of them were lovers.

I slid my key in the front door of Carlton's home, holding my breath along the way. He had given me a key but I had vowed I would never use it without letting him know I was coming. I guessed that was the first lie I had told him in our relationship. The radio was blasting R. Kelly's "Sex Me," and the lights were dim. As I stepped over Carlton's clothes—scattered across the living room floor—I knew exactly how this was about to end. Along the path to his bedroom I stepped over the hot pink heels that had been dropped, undoubtedly in the heat of passion, alongside a black spandex dress and red lace thongs. I could hear the moans and grunts before I reached the bedroom door.

I stood in the hallway, with my mouth open but no words available. I watched Carlton as the muscles tightened in his legs, looking almost unbearable, as he moved back and forth; pumping in and out. Even from my place outside the door I could see his glistening skin as it glowed from his perspiration. I felt my stomach curl in a tight knot as I suppressed my urge to drive my fist through the wall. Certainly Karma had her ugly little hands wrapped around me. Was this how Lisa felt? I continued to watch in awe and sheer disgust as Carlton grabbed the long blonde wig and pulled, causing his lover's back to arch instantly. His mouth opened as his head flew back in ecstasy.

"Shiitt!" He screamed. He pulled out, allowing his juice to spray his lover's back. I cleared my throat gently but loud enough for the two of them to hear. Their heads turned almost simultaneously as they realized that they had been caught. Carlton immediately reached for his pants while Gabe stood straight, adjusting his wig while smiling at me.

# Chapter 36

## Gabe

The trouble with some women is that they refuse to look at obvious clues and signs when it comes down to their men. They walk through their relationships with imaginary blinders on and shades covering their faces to protect their eyes. Their ears are plugged from the truth even when it's screaming and damn near shaking their ass to pay attention. I endured three marriages to women who had this destructive state of mind. I think it was my last wife Carolyn, who was woman enough to admit her downfalls and that she had chosen to make a life with a man whom could never be committed. She never came out and said the words, "I think you're gay" but the look was there in her eyes. Of course, catching me watching gay porn on multiple occasions probably helped fuel that notion. I'm not saying she was correct. I don't like to label myself: I'm a man who loves and loves well. Sometimes I may be in love with a woman; other times it may be a man. I'm a lover and that is exactly what it is.

When I met Carlton I knew that our bond was one that would defy all logic and reasoning. For the first time I felt the longing and desire to please someone other than myself; unselfishly. He was the first man that I allowed access to my body and my heart and I did so with no questions asked. I accepted his fling with Lisa without protest because I knew that it was only that—a fling. A fling that unfortunately resulted in pregnancy and Carlton marrying the wretched wench, but that's how it all started; as a fling. When Carlton advised Lisa that he was involved with another woman when they met, he was referring to me. I pride myself on the fact that I'm able to be whom and whatever he needs. If he wants long flowing hair and high heels, I give him that. If he wants a Caesar cut and Timberlands, I give him that. That's what you do for the person you love. You adjust to fulfill their needs and desires. I didn't give a damn that he also needed a piece of pussy from time to time because the truth remains that he always returned to me and I liked my share of twat occasionally too. However, when he became involved with Toi, I felt enough was enough. One moment he was with me, the next he was with her. When she cut him off he ran back to me. When she said she wanted him, he told me to get over it. I had nothing to do with Lisa discovering Carlton's affair with Toi but when she did, I saw it as an opportunity. Why not pin the two women against each other and start an all-out war? So I started verbally harassing Toi and sent her the gift of the snake. I broke out the window, and yes, I keyed Carlton's car, however that was simply to remind him of what I was capable of. I even went as far as to send Lisa the instant messages and yes, the panties belonging to me. Lisa thought that Nesha was the one who texted her, telling her that Carlton was at the hotel with Toi but Nesha was completely innocent in the whole scheme, she just happened to be at my place when Lisa called the phone and she innocently answered when I told her to. When Lisa assumed that Nesha sent the text, I rolled with it. I know that Nesha has somewhat of a crush on Carlton but she loves Quinton more and she would never betray his trust. Besides,

Carlton wouldn't fuck her even if she was willing, she's not his type.

My plan was perfect. The problem, however, was that Carlton chose what had to be two of the most nervous bitches in the world. They both had major balls when it came to talking shit, but neither one of them knew how to get their hands dirty. I thought Lisa would step up and finally bring Toi to an end, but even she was only as good as a phone call and a total let down when she threw in the towel and signed the divorce papers. I knew I had to handle things myself. So I did. Some might say that my choices and decisions were extreme. I say those people can kiss my sweet black ass.

# Epilogue

## Toi

I know what goes around comes right back around but damn! Another female I can handle but there is no way around catching your man with another man. As it turned out, Nesha had nothing to do with all of the drama and it was Gabe all along. I would have been flattered if my original notion had been true, he wanted me and therefore he was a hater but the man wanted Carlton. Not only did he want him but it was obvious that he had him. Carlton tried desperately to explain and apologize but there are some things I can't forgive. My man digging out another man happens to be one of them. After I called Lisa and told her what I discovered, she advised me that she had no clue that Carlton was on the down-low and she probably never would have known if I hadn't come along. She sounded relieved and hurt at the same time. I apologized to her for my part in any pain she may have been caused.

"Don't worry about it," she said lightly. "I'd say we're even."

"I guess,"

"Karma can be bitch," she sighed.

"True," I agreed. "In this case her name was Gabe."

# Mz. Robinson

Mz. Robinson, born in Huntsville, Alabama is a licensed Realtor and the author of the tantilizing Love, Lies, and Lust Series. Mz. Robinson is an avid reader and advocate for literacy. Although, she began writing as a child, it was not until much later in life that she began to pen short stories. After falling in love with the characters she created, she turned one of her short stories into her debut novel: What We Won't Do For Love. After completing her first manuscript, Mz. Robinson took a break from writing to pursue other career opportunities. Five years later deciding to pursue her passion, she secured a home with G Street Chronicles. Today Mz. Robinson has seven published novels. When she's not writing Mz. Robinson enjoys reading and shopping. She is currently working on her next title and other projects.

G
STREET Essence

# The Love, Lies & Lust Series

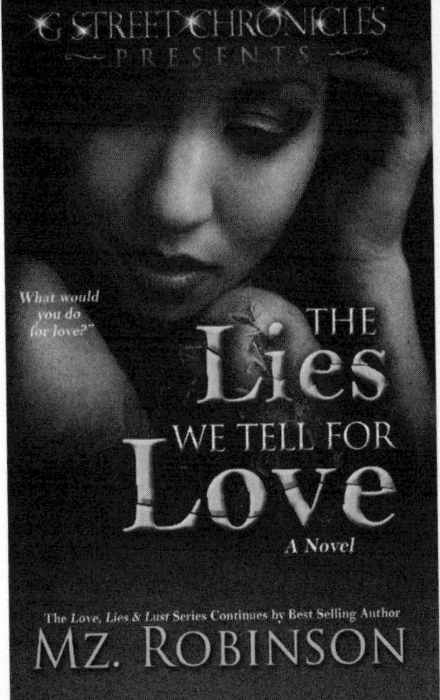

G STREET CHRONICLES
PRESENTS
Platinum Diva
SERIES
G
DIAMOND
MZ. ROBINSON
AUTHOR OF THE "LOVE, LIES & LUST" SERIES
G STREET Essence

G STREET CHRONICLES
PRESENTS
Platinum Diva
SERIES
G
IMANI
MZ. ROBINSON
AUTHOR OF THE "LOVE, LIES & LUST" SERIES
G STREET Essence

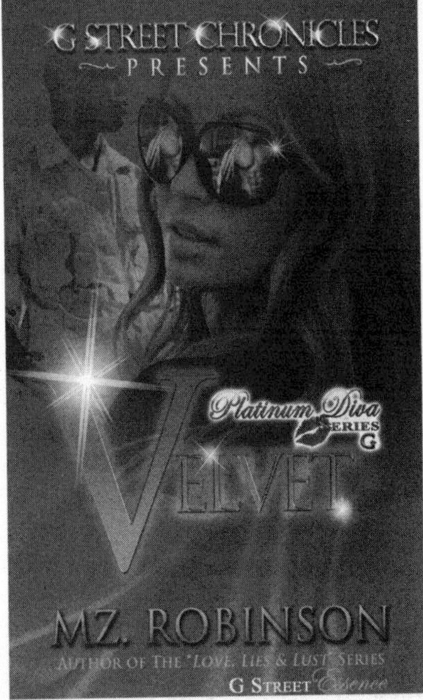
G STREET CHRONICLES
PRESENTS
Platinum Diva
SERIES
G
VELVET
MZ. ROBINSON
AUTHOR OF THE "LOVE, LIES & LUST" SERIES
G STREET Essence

G STREET CHRONICLES
Platinum Diva
SERIES
G
ALEXIS
MZ. ROBINSON
AUTHOR OF THE "LOVE, LIES & LUST" SERIES
G STREET Essence

G STREET CHRONICLES
A NEW URBAN DYNASTY
WWW.GSTREETCHRONICLES.COM